*A
Harlequin
Romance*

OTHER
Harlequin Romances
by ELIZABETH HOY

Many of these titles are available at your local bookseller,
or through the Harlequin Reader Service.

For a free catalogue listing all available Harlequin Romances,
send your name and address to:

HARLEQUIN READER SERVICE,
M.P.O. Box 707, Niagara Falls, N.Y. 14302.
Canadian address: Stratford, Ontario, Canada.

or use order coupon at back of book.

IT HAPPENED IN PARIS

by

ELIZABETH HOY

HARLEQUIN BOOKS

TORONTO   •   WINNIPEG

First published in 1970 by Mills & Boon Limited,
17 - 19 Foley Street, London, England

SBN 373-01538-0

© Elizabeth Hoy 1970

Harlequin Canadian edition published November, 1971
Harlequin U.S. edition published February, 1972

Printed in Canada

1538

CHAPTER ONE

"I AM in Paris", Molly Winston told herself, letting the words form slowly, importantly in her mind, as startling and clear as if they had been spoken aloud. Here she was walking through the Tuileries Gardens, on her way to have lunch with Martin Varney. It didn't seem quite real. The towering chestnut trees on either side of the wide avenue down which she walked were lit with a thousand flowering candles. Pink and white petals littered the ground, making a delicate carpet for the pattering feet of the lovesick doves and pigeons who ran after each other cooing amorously. But it was a morning made for love. Springtime in Paris! Even the fish in the round pond Molly had passed a few moments ago had seemed, contrary to all fish lore, to be pairing; great golden carp, like flashing jewels in the clear water, swimming so closely side by side that Molly was sure they must be holding fins! She had smiled to herself at the whimsical fancy with an odd ache at her heart. Because everything was so much too beautiful this morning, and beauty did not last. 'Beauty whose hand is ever at its lips, bidding farewell.'

If only this walk through the Tuileries could last for ever, an oasis of green and quietness away from the endless roar of the Paris traffic! Was she dreading the meeting with Martin? she wondered. She hadn't seen him for nearly two years, when she had been foolishly and childishly in love with him. She could remember the pain when he had been whisked away from the *Clarion* office in Fleet Street, to work as that well established London daily's correspondent in New York.

Soon after his departure she too had left her job as secretary to J. H. Prendergast, the *Clarion*'s chief leader page editor, to nurse her mother through a long and serious illness. During those dark months she hadn't had much time to think about Martin, or to miss the lively atmosphere of the *Clarion*. But in the forcing-house of the sickroom she had grown up, put her hero-worship of Martin Varney behind her, and for the first time had experienced life as the sequence of harsh realities it so often is. It had come to her that brilliant and ambitious newspaper correspondents do not fall in love with a humble shorthand-typist, even if they did, on occasion, take that shorthand-typist to the theatre—simply to use up a redundant complimentary ticket. It was not perhaps a great surprise; she had never really believed they did, nursing her hopeless passion. How silly it had been, she thought now, as she walked through the bright May morning. It would be interesting to meet Martin in a more sensible and adult frame of mind. She felt suddenly light and carefree. It was wonderful to think of her mother, almost fully restored to health, and now on a convalescent trip to Australia by sea, to stay with Molly's married elder sister.

Following the careful directions Martin had given her over the phone, she exchanged the peace of the gardens for the turmoil of the Rue de Rivoli, made her way along the Rue Castiglione, crossed the wide Place Vendôme with its golden statue of Jeanne d'Arc on horseback, and came to the Rue de la Paix. Was this famous street still the centre of world fashion? Whatever doubts there might be about its status in the jealous and fickle world of *haute couture* the frocks and jewellery displayed behind its plate glass windows were enough to make any normal woman's pulses beat faster. Molly, lingering over them as long as she dared, felt once more that odd reluctance for the approaching reunion. But she had always been a little intimidated...overawed ...by Martin; that perhaps had been part of his fascination for her.

She had, she saw, reached the Place de l'Opéra, and there was the Café de la Paix before her, just as Martin had said it would be, its pavement terrace set out with little tables under gay umbrellas. Most of the tables seemed to be occupied, a hum of lively conversation filled the air. Molly gazed about her, searching for Martin, feeling a little lost.

"Hullo, infant! So you found your way all right?"

Her heart jumped. "Oh, hullo, Martin!"

He was holding her hand in his cool strong grasp, drawing her over to the table he had reserved on the crowded terrace. It was littered, Molly saw, with the international journals he had been reading while he waited for her, the Paris edition of the *Clarion* conspicuous among them.

"How nice to see you! What will you have to drink?" he said, all in one breath.

In a whirl at the sight of him, Molly could think of nothing more exciting than sherry. While he ordered it she studied him. He was just the same as he had been, she registered with satisfaction. The same unruly dark hair with a lock that flopped over his forehead, the thin face with its slight irregularities was as quick and mobile as ever. His mouth, that could so often have a cynical twist to it, smiled as he turned to her. His penetrating all-seeing dark eyes—a newspaperman's eyes— summed her up. A searching glance that made her feel a little nervous—as if she had something to hide from him. You couldn't fool Martin Varney. Fleet Street had long ago sharpened his perceptions, knocked all the nonsense out of him. There was nothing soft or sentimental about him. Or at least that was the impression he gave on the surface, and it was one that Molly had

7

always accepted at face value. A clear-headed, determined young man who knew just where he was going and would let nothing stand in his way.

She said now, sipping her sherry, "I was absolutely flabbergasted when you phoned me last night. How did you know I was in Paris, working for Solita Gerard?"

He grinned. "I have my spies." And then in answer to her look of growing mystification: "It was quite simple really. I was over in the London office the other day and Prendy happened to mention that you had come over to Paris to take a job of sorts. I was glad to hear you were back in circulation once more, and that your mother had made a satisfactory recovery ... due no doubt to your able nursing."

"Not altogether," Molly disclaimed. "But I hope I helped. It was mostly due to some new discovery about the behaviour of blood cells that the research boys have come up with."

"Well, that's good news indeed," he interrupted. It was clear that his interest in sick mothers was flagging. He gave Molly another of his piercing glances. "But why La Gerard?" he asked. "I should have thought you would have returned to your old haunts on the *Clarion*."

"I should have liked to," Molly agreed. "But Mr Prendergast has another secretary now—naturally. I could hardly expect him to have kicked her out for my sake. He did offer me a place in the typing pool when I went to see him. But," she shrugged, dismissing typing pools, "I wasn't keen."

"So you found your way to Solita Gerard instead. How? Is she a friend of yours?" Uncompromising newspaperman's questions.

"No, she isn't a friend," Molly said. "In fact, I have to admit that I'd never heard of her or her famous paintings until my Great-Uncle John Pembury, knowing I was at a loose end, wrote to ask if I would like a summer in Paris, giving a little light assistance to a Miss Gerard, one of his clients. My uncle," she added in parenthesis, "is an art dealer, with a gallery in the Rue de la Seine, the Fontaine. From time to time, I gather, he helps Miss Gerard to sell her paintings...."

"So Pembury is your great-uncle," Martin broke in, sounding a little surprised perhaps at her association with one of the best known art connoisseurs in Paris. "I've met him, of course, in the line of duty. A remarkable old boy. Solita's lucky to have been taken under his wing."

"It seems she had been ill," Molly began.

"Ill?" The query was flung at her on an odd note of alarm.

"It wasn't anything very serious, Uncle Pembury said. Some sort of mild heart attack. Anyway she didn't want to be quite alone at nights in her big apartment on the Rue de la Marne—her daily maid goes home after serving the evening meal. So she happened to ask Uncle John if he knew of some nice, unobtrusive, sympathetic English girl who would like a few weeks in Paris as her companion, in return for pocket money and a good deal of freedom. Naturally I jumped at it."

"Nice, unobtrusive and sympathetic," Martin echoed, lifting a quizzical eyebrow. "And what, more exactly, does your function entail?"

"I haven't discovered yet," Molly replied. "I only arrived the evening before last."

"A heart attack," Martin mused. "I can't imagine Solita having such a thing, unless it's the result of some nervous complication. She did, I know, have some kind of breakdown in health last year ... had to give up her painting for a time."

"She's a friend of yours, then?" Molly asked, a little taken aback, though she couldn't have said why.

"I met her when I was in New York." The rapier glance was veiled as he spoke and in the silence that followed his admission something remained unspoken. After a moment he went on: "She has an apartment off Fifth Avenue, though her family home is in Chicago; yet you could hardly call her American. One of her grandparents was English, the other French—hence the surname Gerard.

"More truly cosmopolitan than expatriate," he murmured to himself after another short pause.

So he knew her well enough to be well versed in her family background.

"She's giving an exhibition of her paintings shortly at my uncle's gallery," Molly said.

Martin nodded. "So I hear. Do you happen to know which of her pictures she'll be showing? She's been through so many phases within the last few years, one wonders which of them is going to stick and become her recognised style. Some of her work has been pretty derivative—those Gauguinesque Solomon Islanders, for example." He dismissed them with a shrug.

"I've seen them," Molly said, and forbore to add that she had taken a violent dislike to them on sight.

"I'm told she has recently gone over to rather strange surrealist stuff. Perhaps you could do a little quiet investigating for me ... find out what she's working on now, perhaps even get me a preview of the pictures she's going to show at your uncle's gallery. I'd like to give her a preliminary write-up in the *Clarion*."

Molly's heart sank. Was this why he had sought her out ... asked her to lunch?

"Wouldn't it be better if you approached her yourself," she suggested, "since you know her? I'm sure she would be pleased at your interest in her work."

Martin shook his head. "I'm hardly on visiting terms at the moment with the temperamental Gerard."

Why this unusual diffidence in a thrustful newspaper man? Molly's clear grey eyes were full of questions. Martin's dark eyes met them, and slid away.

"Don't let it be a bother to you," he went on. "But if the chance arises you could perhaps drop her a hint that I'd like to see her pictures before the show. If you can't manage that have a look at them yourself, so that you could give me some idea what to expect. I wouldn't need very much to provide me with material for my preliminary puff, and it would be, in however small a way, a bit of a journalistic scoop. Solita happens to be news in certain quarters just now."

Molly's heart dropped another notch. So it *was* news he was after! A privileged preview of Solita's pictures. But why couldn't he just ask her for it? It was all very puzzling.

"I'm not very well up in modern painting," she said. "I mean, I wouldn't know which of Solita's pictures were surrealist and which weren't. My knowledge of art just about takes in old-timers like Rubens and Renoir."

"Who were more than two hundred years apart," Martin murmured. "But the alliteration is nice." And then, abruptly, "You've surely seen some of Solita's work already, formed some kind of opinion, suffered a reaction..."

Molly laughed irreverently. "Suffered is about right! Those terrifying Solomon Islanders! They're all over the apartment. The moment you walk in at the hall door you're confronted with a corridor lined with them; warriors armed with spears, witch doctors in weird regalia."

But Martin didn't join in the laughter, and refusing to be sidetracked said, "Haven't you seen any of her more recent work?"

Molly shook her head blankly. "I expect she keeps

that in her studio; a big light room at the end of the corridor. I haven't yet been invited into it."

"How do you get on with Solita?" The sudden change of subject, and the sharp way Martin put the question, were somehow disconcerting.

"I've hardly had time to find out," Molly said. "She's very charming to me ... on the surface." (And why make that reservation? she wondered). "After all, we've only just met. She's very, very lovely."

"She's that all right," Martin agreed, but his mouth went tight and hard.

Summoning a waiter, he paid for the drinks. They were lunching, it emerged, at a restaurant in a nearby side-street, the Mirabeau. It was small and intimate, with an expensive aura, and the food was a culinary dream. They sat side by side on a velvet banquette. Molly gazed in bewilderment at the enormous menu card, written by hand in blotchy violet ink. Martin, leaning over her shoulder, guided her through the maze of dishes. The smoked salmon, he told her, was a *specialité de la maison*, so was the Poulet Lyonnais. They drank a cold dry white wine throughout the meal, which ended with a strawberry soufflé that melted in the mouth. Martin, man-like, concentrated on his food, and conversation was casual. To keep it going Molly enthused about her walk through the Tuileries Gardens; the chestnut trees, the pigeons and doves, the amorous carp. . . .

"You've got your natural history a little mixed," Martin laughed. "Fish, we're told, are incapable of feeling the tender passion. Hence the saying 'Poor fish' !"

"Well, these carp were literally holding each other's fins," Molly insisted, "going round and round the pond in a sort of joyful springtime dance."

Martin's laughter rang out once again. "Here you

are in Paris," he marvelled, "with the wonders of the world all about you and you get steamed up over chestnuts in blossom and a pond full of golden carp! Oh, Molly, I love you!"

But it was so lightly spoken it couldn't mean a thing. All too soon the final cups of coffee were disposed of and they were out in the sunny street saying goodbye.

"Won't you let me call you a taxi?" Martin suggested. "Why you insist upon walking everywhere I can't imagine."

"I like to walk," she assured him. "It's the best way of really getting to know Paris." She did not add that in this city taxis were prohibitively expensive, and her salary at Miss Gerard's was not exactly munificent. She had to keep a careful eye on her francs.

"Well, at least you can walk back a different way," he advised. "Go down past the Madeleine, which will take you into the Rue Royale and across Concorde back to your Tuileries." He gave her a card with his office telephone number. "Give me a call during the next day or two about that preview ..."

"Are you sure it wouldn't be better for you to contact Miss Gerard yourself?" Molly tried again, feeling more and more awkward over her role as intermediary.

"No, it wouldn't be better," Martin said firmly. "La Gerard is quite capable of slamming down her telephone receiver to snub an intrusive newspaperman." He held out his hand in farewell, cutting short her thanks for the delicious lunch—a bribe to procure her services over the preview! She smothered the unworthy thought, but her face was clouded as she walked away from him.

Outside the church of the Madeleine a flower woman sat under a sun-umbrella which sheltered a huge pannier of roses and violets and lilies of the valley. In the Rue de Rivoli the shops were tempting once more, but Molly glanced at them halfheartedly. Just why had Martin

13

Varney invited her to lunch today? Obviously, to talk about Solita Gerard's paintings and enlist her help in getting into the famous studio for a show preview. And why not? Like all newspapermen Martin Varney was an opportunist. It was natural for him to make use of her. After all, they had for a time been office colleagues.

In the Tuileries the pigeons still made love, the children played and the white stone statues stood veiled in the mists of spring greenery. But somehow the morning's magic had gone out of the scene.

Crossing the Pont Solférino Molly stopped to look down at the swiftly moving Seine. Timber and gravel barges of incredible length plied up and down the amber water. There were white pleasure steamers, *bateaux-mouches*, filled with sightseeing tourists. On some of the steamers luncheon on an open foredeck was still being served. It all looked very gay and carefree.

It would be fun to spend a day on one of those white steamers, exploring the upper reaches of the river. If Martin had time perhaps he would take her. He had said over lunch, "You must let me show you around Paris a bit when you have nothing better to do." (As if there could be anything better!) A not very specific offer maybe, but she had a feeling he had meant it. He did not go in for empty politenesses. Leaning her elbow on the sunwarmed parapet, she dreamed of a long hot Sunday on the river with him. She would wear a gay summer frock and a big shady hat. The only drawback to this idyllic picture was that she didn't possess a hat of any kind in the limited wardrobe she had brought with her, and to buy the sort of hat she had in mind in Paris was out of the question. Even the price of a pair of nylons was staggering in this city of soaring inflation.

Reluctant to return just yet to the apartment, she lingered, idle as the occasional solitary fisherman on the banks of the lower *quais*, trailing their lines hopefully in the wake of the fussy steamers. The afternoon was young, she assured herself—Miss Gerard at this hour would be having her after-lunch siesta. There would be nothing to do, Molly thought, but write postcards to the English friends who envied her being in Paris, imagining her to be having a whale of a time. But was she? Would there be enough for her to do at 64b, Rue de la Marne to keep her from boredom? Just how much companionship did Miss Gerard require from her? So far it had consisted mostly of appearing at meals and being around in the evenings after the daily maid, Marie, had gone home. Oh, well, it would all work out, Molly told herself bracingly. Jobs had a knack of developing as you went along.

Crossing the busy Quai Anatole France was a hazard which abruptly ended her reverie. On this one-way thoroughfare cars raced four or five abreast at an alarming speed. The noise was deafening, wrecking the peace of the tree-lined river banks. At intervals the lights changed at the appointed pedestrian crossings, the clear signal lasting so briefly that you had to make an undignified scuttle to get to safety before the merciless cars roared down on you again. Having survived her dicing with death Molly found herself confronted by the solid bulk of the Chamber of Deputies—not nearly so imposing as the London Houses of Parliament, she decided. A short side street took her into the Rue de la Marne. This side of the river was the famous Left Bank with its Bohemian associations; student cafés and arty bistros . . . the Latin Quarter. But here on its perimeter an air of conventionality still prevailed. The Rue de la Marne was wide, its buildings impressively large, its whole air dignified, in spite of a sprinkling of small shops and the inevitable corner *tabac*, where, Molly had discovered, you could drink coffee, buy postcards and stamps and use the public telephone. There was also a

15

drinks counter, invariably propped up by unaccountably idle workmen drinking Pernods or light beer.

The entrance to 64b was uncompromisingly gloomy— a huge wooden gateway, bolted and barred, giving the place the appearance of a fortress under siege. A small wicket gate kept unlocked during daylight hours opened on to a dark cobbled passageway, flanked by the *concierge's* lodge. Suspicious eyes peered from behind muslin blinds as you passed. It was all a little daunting, but not to be taken too seriously, for the *concierge* was really a very harmless, kindly old man, and beyond the cobbled passageway the sun poured down into a beautifully kept courtyard. Here azaleas flowered in ornamental tubs before the silvery façades of two beautiful old town houses, mansions with elegantly shuttered windows, wrought-iron balconies, and curving flights of steps which led to eighteenth-century doorways. Obviously there was wealth in this sunny corner, securely hidden by the powerfully barricaded outer gate, a sanctuary that might have been planned to resist the terrors of the French Revolution. Perhaps it had!

On the sunless side of the little quadrangle the building was of an altogether humbler kind, one large old grey house cut up into fairly spacious flats, one flat to each of the four floors. Miss Gerard's flat was on the top storey, as befitted a painter. She would need her attic studio with its range of north-lit windows.

To reach this eyrie Molly had to take a tiny lift, as narrow and almost as airless as a coffin. It gave her a sense of claustrophobia she had to control as it purred gently upwards. A small dark landing awaited her, flanked by Miss Gerard's front door, which opened on to the long corridor full of the painted witch doctors Molly had mentioned to Martin.

Letting herself in with the key she had been given, she stood a moment, peering through the gloom, trying to remember which of the many doors led to her bedroom. From the canvases on the walls white eyeballs bulged in black faces. There was an immense rubber plant in a bronze tub, its fleshy leaves drooping disconsolately. A revolting botanical specimen, Molly thought privately. All the same she must remember to give the poor thing some water. It looked as if it could do with it. A jungle plant, it couldn't be much fun for it here in this narrow airless corridor. Maybe Solita had installed it to keep the witch doctors company. On the evening she arrived Molly had found them overpowering—not because of their colour, but by the way they were depicted; huge, threatening figures, larger than life, their bulging eyes cold and inimical. They had been painted in fear, rather than love; there was no warmth, no human understanding. Martin had been wrong to compare them with the kindly South Sea islanders of Gauguin—with whose work Molly happened to be familiar because she had a reproduction of one of his Tahiti pictures in her room at home.

From the kitchen, on the right-hand side of the corridor, there came a clatter of dishes, indicating that Marie, the *femme de ménage* was coping rather noisily with the after-lunch washing up. Cutlery rattled, cupboard doors banged; it sounded as if Marie was in a temper about something.

Suddenly the kitchen door opened and she looked out. "Is that you, *mademoiselle*?" she greeted Molly. "Madame is resting in the salon, but she said you were to go to her as soon as you came in..." Breaking off, the woman made a beckoning gesture.

"Come in here a moment, *si vous voulez*!"

Molly followed her into the kitchen. It was clear now that she was indeed in a temper, her usually placid face crimson, her eyes blazing with righteous wrath. Nervously she twisted the glass cloth she held in her

17

hands. "I have been insulted," she burst out. "But mortally! Madame has accused me of bringing the short change when I make the daily shopping. She shouted at me, made me the scene *formidable*, says I have been robbing her consistently ever since I have been with her!" The words choked her. She could not go on for a moment.

In embarrassed silence, Molly tried to think of something soothing she could say. Her French was fairly adequate but not idiomatic, and Marie spoke so rapidly it took a little while to sort out all she had been saying.

"What made Madame suspect you?" Molly brought out at last.

Marie flung out her hands in a Gallic gesture of despair. "Who can say? She is malicious, that one. Herself not to be trusted, her moods going this way and that like a weathercock. So she turns on me in this unreasonable fashion after a year of faithful service. If I was robbing her, why did she not find it out long ago? *Le bon Dieu* knows she scrutinises my shopping lists and the sums I pay out very thoroughly every time I return from the market. Now suddenly she decides, for no reason whatever, that I am a thief. If it is that she wishes to get rid of me, she has her wish. Naturally I could not remain in her service another hour after this. As soon as I have cleared up these dishes I am leaving...."

The service bell above the kitchen door pealed sharply.

"Voilà!" Marie exclaimed. "That will be her ladyship. She will have heard you come in. Anyway you had better go to her. If she is ringing for me she is out of luck. All I want from her is my week's wages—a full week, mind! She can give it to you for me. I am not going near her again. I wouldn't trust myself. And you can tell her so, with my compliments."

The bell pealed impatiently once more.

"I am so sorry all this has happened," Molly murmured inadequately, and went out into the dark corridor feeling increasingly uncomfortable. Marie's story was certainly rather odd . . . if it was strictly true. Was it possible that Miss Gerard would accuse her of dishonesty without clear evidence? After months of faithful service. A woman of moods like a weathercock. Not to be trusted. Hadn't there been a hint of reservation in Martin's tone when he asked 'How do you get on with her?' And he shrank from phoning her to ask simply for a preview of her pictures. Which was not like Martin. Just what sort of woman was thisbeautiful quick-tempered artist, Solita Gerard?

"Come in, my dear," she invited, as Molly hesitated on the threshold of the salon, a long narrow room full of red velvet hangings and old ornate furniture. The settee in the centre of the dusty carpet was as large as a double bed, piled with faded silk-covered cushions. Solita, lying in the middle of them, looked appealingly frail and slender, her thin oval face intense, her eyes shadowy and enormous, heavily made up. Though, according to Uncle John, she was barely thirty she had a burned-out look. This in a strange way emphasised her beauty, perhaps because it was based on a perfect bone structure. Her brow was high, her cheekbones accentuated, her small, straight nose delicate and precise above the full passionate mouth. But it was her eyes that were the dominating feature; a clear green set at an oblique angle which gave her a slightly oriental appearance—eloquent eyes, and yet, Molly suspected, they could hide more than they revealed. Solita Gerard was a sophisticate to her elegant fingertips.

Leaning back amid the cushions she seemed wholly relaxed and at ease. It was impossible to imagine her making a 'scene *formidable*' with her maid.

"I'm so glad you've come back," she said. "Such a tiresome thing has happened. Marie has given me notice and is leaving in a huff." She patted the edge of the settee invitingly. "Do sit down and listen to my tale of woe."

Molly perched herself gingerly on the far end of the settee, raising a little cloud of dust as she did so. It would be understandable if Marie had been reproached for her neglect of the apartment. Even with the help of a morning charwoman nothing much in the way of house cleaning seemed to be achieved. It was evident that the salon hadn't had a thorough turn out for weeks. Yet it maintained a certain musty elegance, perhaps because the furniture and hangings were of an excellent quality, and Solita's pictures were everywhere to distract the eye—landscapes, still life studies, great billowy nudes, with the same bulging eyeballs as the Solomon Islanders. Solita seemed to have a thing about bulging eyeballs.

"Servants are impossible in Paris," she was saying. "I'm so tired of them, doing as little as they can in return for the enormous wages they demand. I've long ago given up hope of Marie reducing the place to any kind of domestic order, but at least she's a first-class cook. And now she's taken offence because I've hinted that she's at times a bit careless in the matter of small change when she does my shopping." Solita sighed pathetically. "Perhaps it's just as well," she said softly. Her great eyes, fixed on Molly, held a calculating gleam. "I can't really afford Marie at the moment. Things are going to be difficult for me until I see how my show goes. Life is so expensive in France, and there's my apartment in New York to keep up as well as this place here."

The calculating look deepened. "People think that because I belong to the wealthy Gerard family of

Chicago that I'm made of money. It's not so. I'm a very junior member of a junior branch of the clan, and with the various economic upheavals in the world my income, like most people's, has suffered."

Molly, thinking a little guiltily of her own so far unearned salary, felt uncomfortable. Just what was Miss Gerard getting at? "If I can be of any help ..." she murmured.

"Oh, but you can!" Solita seized eagerly on the tentative offer. "I thought if you didn't mind we could try managing just with Madame Garcia who comes in to do the rough work in the mornings. If she could give me an extra hour ... produce a simple lunch. She's Spanish, which means she's much cheaper than a French maid ... and I expect she can make herself useful in the kitchen." Solita's beautiful eyes grew dreamy. "Can *you* cook?" she asked softly, almost coaxingly. "Just simple dishes. If you could see to the evening meal ... we wouldn't need anything elaborate."

"But of course, Miss Gerard!" Molly was as genuinely pleased as she sounded. "I seem to have done nothing but drift about idly since I arrived. I should love to feel I was really making myself useful."

"There would be the shopping, which I hate; do you think you could cope with that?"

Molly, who suspected no pitfalls in the question, nodded vigorously. "I should enjoy the shopping, Miss Gerard. ..."

Solita made a small grimace. "I wish you would call me Solita; it's so much more friendly, and I hope we're going to be friends."

Molly glowed. "Thank you, Miss Gerard ... Solita." She crushed the unworthy suspicion that Solita was laying on the charm a bit thickly, deliberately manipulating her, but she didn't mind. It was being done with such sweetness that it was irresistible. A woman of many moods, Marie had said. Perhaps she was, but so far Molly had only encountered her at her fascinating best.

"I cooked for my mother all the time she was ill," Molly said, after a swift mental review of her skills in the kitchen. Would they be enough for the exotic Solita?

She frowned slightly. "Only that I'm not ill, and I hate invalid cooking. That week I had in the nursing home recently when I was supposed to be having a heart attack was enough for me. Steamed fish and baked custards—ugh!"

"I didn't mean I expected to cook invalid dishes for you," Molly hastily corrected. "I only mention them as part of my culinary experience." That sounded so grandiloquent that she went a little pink. "All I'm trying to tell you is that I *can* cook—simply. Plain roasts and vegetables, fruit tarts, scones ... the usual English fare."

"Okay, honey! Spare me the details." Solita yawned behind silver-tinted fingernails, openly bored with the subject of food, although it was she herself who had introduced it. "Just give me good steak fillets and fresh salads, and I'll be content." Her American drawl, subtly emphasised, made her words a dismissal flicked with scorn.

"Incidentally," she went on, gazing at her silver fingernails, "I like my evening meal served about eight, and you will eat it with me. Your mornings will be your own, and you will be free to go out after dinner—so long as you come back here to sleep. I don't want to make a prisoner of you. And obviously there's a boyfriend in the background ... this man you were lunching with today. How did it go?" Her smile was old-fashionedly arch. "Where did he take you?"

"To the Mirabeau." And then hastening to correct the mistaken implications, Molly added, "He's not my boy-friend, just someone I used to know when I worked as a secretary on the London *Clarion*—Martin Varney. I think you've met him."

There was an instant of electrified silence. The green eyes widened, filling with something that might have been fear, until the dropped lashes hid them. Beneath her make-up Solita Gerard had gone rather pale. "Did you say Martin Varney?" she asked in a small voice. "What's he doing in Paris?"

"Working for the *Clarion*. He's their Paris correspondent at the moment."

"That figures." The long green eyes were hard now and wary. If the mention of Martin Varney had for some reason thrown Solita momentarily off balance, she was in control again.

"I remember," she said coolly, "when he left New York last summer he was supposed to be taking up some kind of European assignment. I don't know why... but it didn't occur to me that it might be in Paris."

"He's interested in your forthcoming show at the Fontaine," Molly ventured. "In fact he asked me to find out if you would be willing to allow him to have a preview of the pictures you'll be exhibiting. He said he might be able to get you some preliminary publicity in the *Clarion*."

The effect of this disclosure was unexpected; Solita threw back her head and went off into peals of laughter. What was the joke? Molly wondered in some mystification. Solita's whole reaction to the news of Martin's presence in Paris was puzzling. But Martin too had behaved oddly when Solita's name had been mentioned over the luncheon table. What was there between these two? Surely something more than a casual encounter in the artistic circles of New York.

"A gossip column puff for me," Solita was saying, "and a minor scoop for him—a peep at the Gerard paintings before the rest of the Press get at them. A newspaperman would sell his soul for less."

She turned her brilliant glance on Molly with an air of sudden decision. "Let him have his peep. Ask him to dinner ... tomorrow evening. You can give him some of your plain roast and a nice apple pie. I'm sure he'll be charmed. Ring him now and see if he can make it."

She pushed the telephone, which stood on the table beside her, towards Molly, who hesitated, abashed. The idea of speaking to Martin on the phone in front of Solita for some reason appalled her.

"Go on!" Solita urged. "He can't bite you."

Fishing in the handbag she was still carrying, Molly produced the number he had given her, and with increasing embarrassment proceeded to dial it. Mercifully Martin was not in his office. The girl who answered Molly's enquiry said he had come in for a few moments after lunch, but almost immediately gone out again. It was understood he would not be returning until late afternoon.

Solita muttered a careless *"Tant pis!"* when this was relayed to her. "You can ring him again later on."

And I'll go out and do it privately in the phone box at the *tabac* on the corner, Molly resolved.

"Right now," Solita was continuing, "you'd better take that monster in the kitchen her week's wages, and tell her to clear off. I don't want to set eyes on her again."

Yawning once more, she ran her fingers through her thick dark hair. It was silky and soft, with just the right amount of curl, skilfully cut to fit like a cap about her shapely skull. "I'm going to take a shower," she declared, rolling with languid grace off the settee. "Then I'll put in a couple of hours in my studio. Bring me a cup of coffee there about five o'clock. Before you go out shopping."

"You want something brought in for dinner?" Molly asked, a little bewilderedly. Five o'clock seemed a late hour to be attending to such a detail.

"Of course I want something brought in for dinner," Solita echoed, mimicking Molly's puzzled tone. "Look, baby!" she went on with an exaggerated air of long-suffering. "Do I have to spell everything out to you? We don't eat stale food in France. We buy it an hour or two before serving it. You'll get most of what you need in the Rue de Verneuil just round the corner. This is one of your chores—a daily forage every afternoon for interesting things to eat. Madame Garcia will see to the dull items like bread and milk and wine. You do realise that nothing, but nothing, is delivered by the shopkeepers in France? Everything has to be fetched and carried. *C'est entendu?*"

"Yes, Miss Gerard."

From a drawer in the telephone table Solita produced a roll of notes, which she proceeded to count. "Here are Marie's wages, and a hundred francs for your shopping—not that I expect you to spend anything like that amount on one evening's meal. Let me know when you want some more, and please bring me the bills as you go along. That's one thing I could never persuade Marie to do...one of the circumstances which made me doubt her honesty. They'll always give you a receipt at the shops if you ask for it."

She waved a dismissive hand. "That's all for the moment. Just keep out of my way until dinner time—apart from bringing my coffee, of course. I want to work."

Not a particularly gracious dismissal, but Molly was too busy digesting the spate of instructions to feel resentful.

In the kitchen Marie was putting on her hat and coat,

her round face still red and wrathful. She snatched the money Molly handed to her, and counted it suspiciously. "It's just right, for a wonder!" she pronounced. "Never in my life have I worked for such a mean employer, watching every crumb, every sou! 'Bring me the bills, Marie'," she mocked in a falsetto voice. "And her temper! *Mon Dieu!*" Marie cast her eyes upward. "The times she has turned on me without an instant's notice. One minute all honey, just because she wants something, and the next minute treating me like dirt, shouting at me, calling me names you wouldn't expect from a lady." She picked up her handbag and stuffed her wages into it. "Well, thank goodness I've seen the last of her!"

Molly cast a desperate look round the kitchen. She had better get her bearings before Marie vanished into thin air. "Is that the larder cupboard over there?" she asked. "And does the stove work easily? It is gas, isn't it? I've got to see to the evening meal now you are going," she explained.

"C'est vrai!" Marie exclaimed in astonishment. "Madame is not going to engage another cook?"

"Not while I'm staying with her. She says Madame Garcia can remain a little longer in the mornings, and do the lunches, but I am to make the evening meal."

"What did I tell you!" Marie demanded triumphantly. "She is as mean, that one, as some old peasant woman stuffing her francs away in a stocking under the mattress." She wagged her head. "Oh, I can see it all now! As soon as you came here, giving your services no doubt for a pittance, she decided to get rid of me... use you in the kitchen instead. All this *blague* about me cheating over the shopping is a trumped-up affair. I've been here long enough for her to have found out before if I was a thief. But no!" Marie made a vast gesture.

"She gets rid of me in her own mean fashion, simply for her own advantage. That she robs me of my character matters not at all." She shrugged, throwing Molly a glance of commiseration. "I wish you luck of her, *ma pauvre*!"

Molly, smothering the alarm she felt at this outburst and its implications, saw that Marie was about to leave. "What do you think she would like for dinner tonight?" she asked hurriedly. "She said something about steak."

"Ah, the *biftek*," Marie mused. "This is one of her favourite dishes. See that it is served *sanglant* ... underdone ... and perhaps have some *haricots verts* to go with it, and *sauté* potatoes. For wine there is the Beaune. You will find it in the cold cupboard out on the back landing. It is there we keep our cellar. See that it is at room temperature before it is brought to the table. For the rest," Marie paused a moment to draw a breath, "start with some simple *hors d'oeuvres*, or an avocado pear with a sharp dressing. For dessert Madame likes fresh fruit in season. As for the cheeses. ..." She rattled off a string of names Molly was sure she would never remember.

"I'd better go out at once and get that steak before the butchers' shops close," she said, only to learn that the provision shops in the Rue de Verneuil were scarcely open yet.

"They close at lunch time," Marie explained, "and do not open again until between four and five o'clock, remaining open until nine or thereabouts."

All these different customs! There are deep waters before me, Molly thought apprehensively. Steak *sanglant* that had to be tender ... or else! *Sauté* potatoes. Wine at the correct temperature, the mystery of *hors d'oeuvres*, and all those cheeses with the unpronounceable names. To say nothing of discovering just which shop sold what, and how much one had to pay for day-to-day purchases.

"If you are getting *roblochon*," Marie was saying, "buy it *au nature*; the packaged sort is never so good."

What on earth was *roblochon*? One of those complicated cheeses, Molly supposed.

When Marie had gone she spent some time exploring her domain. Unlike the rest of the apartment the kitchen with its cupboards was in fairly good order. She searched for the wherewithal to make Solita's afternoon coffee and found that it had to be freshly ground. No instant coffee in a self-respecting French cuisine! Promptly at five o'clock she entered the studio with the jug of hot coffee on a tray, flanked by sugar and cream. Solita in a paint-stained overall was standing before an easel making what looked like a series of confused lines and patterns on a large canvas. They made no sense to Molly, but Solita appeared contented and absorbed.

"Leave the tray on the little table over there," she murmured absently, without turning from her work. And then, still more absently, "When you phone Martin tell him to come early tomorrow evening—round about seven-thirty, in time for drinks."

Molly put the tray down on the table indicated— littered with brushes and tubes of paint. She stood hesitant a moment.

"I noticed we're almost out of butter, Miss Gerard," she ventured. "I wondered what kind you prefer, salted or unsalted?"

Solita flung her lump of charcoal down with an angry gesture. "Get what you like!" she shouted rudely. "Only don't bother me about it. Housekeeping details I abominate ... and I'm busy. Why didn't you find out from Marie what sort of butter we buy?"

"I'm sorry, I didn't think of it while she was here ..."

"Well, that's just too bad," Solita drawled. "But ..."

28

her voice rose again, "having taken on the job of seeing to these boring matters for heaven's sakes go and get on with it, and leave me alone!"

Snubbed and inwardly fuming, Molly withdrew. Even if it had not been altogether tactful to talk to Solita about anything so mundane as butter while she was in the throes of creation there was no need to be so offensive. Where now was her sweetness and charm? Having used it to persuade her to take on the cooking, Molly thought, it had been summarily turned off. Just as Marie had said. "One minute she is all honey because she wants something, and the next minute she is treating you like dirt." Molly's uneasiness about her employer increased.

For two pins, she told herself impulsively, she would follow Marie's example—walk out of the apartment and leave Solita to cope alone with her wretched *bifteks* and *roblochons*. Artistic temperament was all very well, but there were limits, and Molly wasn't accustomed to being shouted at and ordered about. Nor was she going to put up with it! After dinner, which she would prepare and serve perfectly, she would tell Solita so. In her mounting indignation it seemed to her that she had made a mistake in coming to act as companion to this unknown woman—and a still more serious mistake in promising to take on the cooking. But there was still time to draw back. She would just have to tell Solita she had changed her mind.

"There are certain aspects of working for you which I did not suspect until I actually began my duties," she would say ambiguously, but pointedly and with the greatest of dignity. "I've come to the conclusion that I'm not fitted to cope with your housekeeping, and had much better go back to England and return to my customary secretarial employment."

But she knew in her heart that she would not return to England, nor would her fine speech of resignation be made. At least not just now. Tomorrow evening Martin was coming to dinner and more than anything in the world she wanted to see him with Solita ... find out if she could what their relationship might be.

CHAPTER TWO

ONCE out in the Rue de Verneuil the annoying exchange with Solita began to seem less important. The scene all about her was so animated and novel that it took Molly out of herself completely. If this was shopping in one of the back streets of Paris, it was fun! The narrow pavements were thronged with excited shoppers, everybody seeming to be passionately absorbed in the business of selecting what they wanted from the tempting array of food displayed. Fruit and vegetables spilled over from the greengrocers' open-fronted windows in a riot of colour; strawberries, cherries, melons and peaches; artichokes, aubergines, tight little Italian cauliflowers, baby marrows—those delicious courgettes—tomatoes as large as grapefruit.

French voices rose in a rippling fountain of sound. Hands waved and gesticulated. Workmen in blue overalls pushed their way among the throng carrying oil-cloth bags bursting with bottles of wine. Women in tight-bosomed black frocks, bare-headed, their hair done in tight buns on the tops of their heads, hugged long crisp loaves. Younger, smarter women, probably on their way home from offices or shops, carried baskets and bags filled to the brim with good things to eat.

"*Ensuite! Ensuite!*" called the distracted shopkeepers to the tangle of customers in the small *crêmeries, charcuteries* and *épiceries*. Nowhere was there anything so orderly as a queue.

Molly bought the avocado pears (which would be easier to handle than the *hors d'oeuvres* tonight) and was shocked to find they cost almost seven shillings each.

The price of the steak was equally staggering and the butter cost at least twice as much as it would have done in England. It wasn't difficult to remember to ask for the receipts for these purchases. She would have done so in sheer self-protection, without Solita's admonition.

Yet so many of the people surging around her were poorly and shabbily dressed, most of them obviously workers or humble housewives. How did they afford these high prices? It remained a mystery which Molly was never to solve. Even the confectioners and pastry-cooks were crowded with drab-looking folk buying the mouth-watering wares displayed—with their exorbitant price tickets. Sniffing the delicious odours of chocolate, vanilla and cream, Molly contented herself with buying a few *croissants* for the next morning's breakfast—a mistake, she was to discover. *Croissants* were only eaten fresh from the oven—never, never kept overnight.

By the time she had finished her shopping there was a large hole in the hundred-franc note. At this rate it would not last more than a couple of days. She would have to be more careful in future, though she honestly felt she had stuck to necessities today.

Waking the next morning, she lay drowsily for a few moments, savouring a feeling of well-being and happy anticipation. Something nice was going to happen to-day. Then she remembered: Martin was coming to dinner. She had phoned him yesterday evening—from the *tabac* as she had planned—and this time he was in his office.

"Thanks, infant, you've done well," he commended her, when she gave him Solita's invitation. "I'll be along at seven-thirty, as ever is!" He had rung off then, cutting short the possibility of any further conversation. Molly had half expected that he might want to ask more questions about Solita and her paintings—but no

32

doubt he had thought he could satisfy his curiosity more directly now that he was visiting the apartment.

She would cook the best possible English meal for him, she resolved. It would be a change for him after the exotic French dishes she imagined to be his daily fare.

Her own attempts at a Frenchified repast hadn't been bad last night. At least Solita hadn't grumbled. She had, indeed, gone out of her way to be friendly, chatting amiably throughout the meal, perhaps to make up for her outburst of ill temper earlier on.

When Molly told her she had contacted Martin, and that he would be pleased to come to dinner, she dropped her long lashes and for a moment once more there was that oddly charged silence Molly had noticed when she first mentioned Martin's name. Recovering herself, she had said a little too casually, "Oh, good, I'm glad he can make it," and at once began to talk about something else.

Now, glancing at her bedside clock, Molly saw that it was half-past eight. In a few moments Madame Garcia would be bringing in a breakfast tray. This breakfast in bed routine was an unwonted luxury, but Solita had decreed it. "I don't like my guests wandering about the place much before noon," she had declared, "nor do I do much wandering myself. I'm not really human until I've had lunch."

So she was to be a guest during the morning hours, Molly reflected with amusement, and a cook-housekeeper from late afternoon onwards! That gave her a long free morning in which she could go out, explore the parks, the galleries, the shops. It wouldn't matter if she were in for lunch or not, Solita had told her, so long as she warned Madame Garcia beforehand. So really, all things considered, and if Solita behaved herself, it wasn't going to be too difficult a job.

33

And there was always Martin in the background. Hastily Molly suppressed *that* particular line of thought.

This was one hour of the day when sunshine poured into her attic bedroom for a brief time. She liked her little room, and would like it better when she had persuaded Madame Garcia to sweep some of the fluff from under the divan bed! Meanwhile she would enjoy the steam radiator which tempered the chill of a May morning, the big hand basin with its constant supply of hot water and the deep window under its fairytale mansard roof. There was a wide ledge just beneath it where pigeons talked to one another in dulcet tones.

This morning they had been driven away by the strange noises, loud bangs and bumps from the courtyard below, which sounded as if someone was throwing planks of wood from one end of the enclosure to the other. Molly wondered what was going on, but before she had time to get out of bed and look, Madame Garcia appeared with breakfast.

Madame Garcia, one of the many Spaniards who exile themselves to Paris in search of work, was small and thin and eternally harassed, talking a strange *patois* of her own, which she fondly believed to be French. It wasn't easy to understand her, but she was so gentle and sweet and anxious to please that language difficulties didn't seem to matter. In a peculiar and almost miraculous fashion she and Molly contrived to communicate.

This morning she was jubilant at the prospect of working longer hours in the apartment, presumably for extra pay. "And I am to have lunch here!" she added with such open delight that Molly guessed guiltily that she didn't always have enough to eat. (Those fantastic food prices in the shops!)

There was a louder than ever bang from the courtyard as she placed the tray on the bedside table. Workmen had arrived, Madame Garcia struggled to explain,

34

to paint the woodwork and pipes on the exterior of the building. The window frames too were to be done. They would, it emerged, start this job at the top floor and were already putting up scaffolding and a catwalk. "The Señorita had better keep her curtains drawn," Madame Garcia advised as she departed.

But the sunshine was so pleasant that Molly decided to leave the curtains as they were, pulled back to admit the sunshine. It would surely take the workmen some time before the scaffolding was completed.

She had finished her breakfast and was pottering about her room in a flimsy dressing gown when the young man appeared at her open window. With a startled glance she became aware of a pleasant young face topped by a mop of reddish-brown hair. "*Bonjour, madame!*" this apparition greeted her politely.

"*Bonjour,*" Molly responded automatically. How on earth had they put up their catwalk so quickly? But she realised she had been reading a gripping Agatha Christie over her prolonged breakfast and she supposed the time had slipped by.

"*Il fait beau ce matin,*" the young man offered conversationally, producing a scraper which he began to apply with some vigour to the window frame.

Molly's reply to this comment upon the weather was a firm step towards the window where she drew the curtains together with a dismissive swish.

"*Excusez-moi,*" a crestfallen voice sounded beyond this cretonne barrier. "Perhaps it would be more *convenable* if I were to do this window frame another time."

"Certainly it would!" Molly snapped.

The young man with another apology melted away so silently that he might have taken wings and floated off over the sunny depths of the courtyard below.

Giggling over the silly encounter, Molly went along the corridor to have a leisurely morning bath, another

35

perquisite of the job at 64b Rue de la Marne. The bathroom was as neglected as every other room in the apartment, but the bath was large and new, the supply of hot water more than adequate and there were lots of soft fluffy towels and great jars of perfumed bath powder to give a sense of luxury. It was wonderful to be able to take her time in this way at an hour when normally she would already be at work in some office.

When finally she was ready to go out she made her way to the Rue de la Seine to call upon Great-Uncle Pembury. He was pleased to see her, but he hadn't much time in which to talk to her, as clients came and went in his elegant picture gallery. "Is Solita treating you well?" he asked sharply at one point.

Molly, guardedly, said she was.

"Well, keep her up to it!" Uncle John replied firmly. "She can be a bit of a tartar when the mood takes her, and she's quite unpredictable in her likes and dislikes. As long as she has taken to you it should be all right," he ended hopefully.

This, Molly felt, was hardly the moment to tell him she had undertaken to cook what was the most important meal of the day in any French household. She had an idea he wouldn't approve and there was no use in complicating matters. It wasn't as if she were going to be in Paris for long—just a few summer weeks. Her attempt at French housekeeping was a challenge she would enjoy—as long as she didn't take Solita and her tantrums too seriously.

This evening she would be cooking not for Solita but for Martin.

She walked home down the Boulevard St Germain where cafés with famous names, which had once been the sanctuary of the world's literati, were now filled with tourists and turbulent students. Not that there was any sign of trouble on this sunny morning, apart from the occasional blunt-nosed police wagon hurrying on its way, sounding its unceasing two-note warning. Difficult to believe on this peaceful spring day in the stories of student demonstrations and riots.

Back at the apartment she found that Solita had eaten an early lunch and gone off to the hairdresser's. In the sunless *salle-à-manger* Molly sat down to a solitary meal. Madame Garcia, popping in and out with the various dishes, was inclined to be talkative, enlarging on the enormities of the workmen's intrusion. Figures in overalls passed up and down the catwalk beyond the window as she talked.

"How long does this redecorating take?" Molly asked when Madame Garcia appeared with the cheese and fruit.

Only God knew, she answered ominously. "They are to do the inside of the window frames as well as the outside, one understands. So that soon they will be indoors, all over the place." She threw up her hands and rolled her eyes in Spanish abandon.

Once more alone Molly looked about her, wondering how she could cheer this desolate room up a bit before Martin arrived. The walls, which had not been painted for years by the look of them, were a drab mustard colour, the curtains made of dusty dark red velvet, and Solita seemed to have hung up a series of her most depressing paintings; still life mostly—dead game bleeding on kitchen tables, an equally dead cluster of herrings lying beside an enormous butcher's knife, which, presumably, would be used to gut them. The furniture, all of heavy dark wood of some kind, was in need of polishing, especially the enormous sideboard on which stood an array of tarnished silver, including a lidless soup tureen filled with old bills and letters, and a Brittany fruit bowl containing a few bad apples and three cumbersome iron keys.

Molly wished she had asked Madame Garcia to give the place a bit of a turn out this morning, but she was hardly yet on a footing in the little household which would justify her in giving orders to the maid, and Solita didn't seem to mind what the place looked like. But artists were apt to be undomesticated. Odd that people dedicated to the production of beauty could be blind to the squalor of their surroundings. But that, so often, was how it was. At least she could buy some flowers for the table, Molly planned—if the francs held out.

Solita had not returned from her visit to the hairdresser when she went out to her evening shopping. The leg of lamb, or *gigot* as she had discovered it was called, took almost all that was left of the hundred francs. She had to draw on her own slender supply of cash to buy the apples for the pie. There was nothing left with which to get flowers. The few remaining coins in her purse had to be spent on string beans and potatoes.

Overloaded, she made her way homewards, and approaching the formidable entrance to 64b found herself face to face with the chestnut-haired window painter. Tall and limber, there was a certain grace and dignity about him, even in paint-stained jeans. He gave her a courtly bow, *"Bo'soir, madame!"*

"Bo'soir," she murmured abstractedly. Hampered by her purchases, she looked at the great wooden gateway confronting her. She would have to put some of her parcels down before she had a hand to spare to push the electric button which manipulated the small wicket gate."

"Permettez!" the young man cried, springing to her aid, and when he had opened the wicket for her, he firmly relieved her of the heaviest of her baskets. Somehow after that she was walking with him along the cobbled passageway, thanking him for his kindness.

"You are English," he said, speaking in that tongue. "Is it that you have come to Paris, *peut-être*, to make the *cuisine* for Madame Gerard?" (Had he been gossiping with Madame Garcia?)

"You could put it like that," Molly answered this rather too personal question, and saw him puzzle over the idiomatic phrase.

"*Au pair*," he summed it up triumphantly, after a moment's contemplation.

"Well, I suppose that about covers it," Molly conceded, deliberately being obscure.

"*Tiens!*" sighed the young man. "But you speak what is for me the too advanced English. Anyway you are here, and that is nice for you, I hope." He gave her a dazzling smile. He was really quite good-looking, Molly decided, and had very charming manners—apart from being a little bit too curious about her affairs. In his late teens, she decided—with the youthful appeal of a friendly puppy.

"Permit me to introduce myself," he said as Molly rang for the lift. Drawing himself up to his full height, gave her another of his courtly little bows and said, "André Colbert, at your service."

"How do you do, Monsieur Colbert?" Molly murmured formally, wishing the lift would hurry up and descend.

"Me, I am André, please," the young man said. "Monsieur Colbert is my father, foreman of the firm in which I am apprenticed; learning the business from the feet up."

"From the bottom up," Molly corrected.

"The bottom." André sounded a little shocked. "That is how you say it in English ... the *derrière*?"

Molly laughed in spite of herself. "Not that kind of bottom. The beneath," she experimented. "*En bas.*"

She pointed to the ground and then up into the air. "The bottom from which one climbs to the top."

"Ah! *C'est entendu!*" André breathed, greatly relieved. "I learn the business from the bottom to the top," he repeated proudly, as if he had collected a difficult piece of idiomatic English.

After that it was impossible to go on treating him distantly. When the lift appeared he got into it with her, insisting that he must carry the heavy basket up to the apartment. It was a pretty tight squeeze. André Colbert seemed all at once to be impossibly broad-shouldered and tall. Jammed together in the tiny space they looked at one another over the *gigot* of lamb and the beans and potatoes. André's amber brown eyes held a glint of mischief. *"C'est bien, ce petit ascenseur, n'est-ce pas?"* he said softly. Which freely translated could have meant, "It is a bit of all right, this little lift, don't you think?"

Molly, assuming a sternly correct demeanour, pretended not to have understood, and anyhow they were bumping to a halt at the fourth floor, where André, still refusing to be separated from the shopping basket, carried it into the kitchen.

Solita was standing by the stove brewing herself her afternoon coffee. Fresh from her session in a beauty parlour she was more glamorous than ever, her hair newly washed and set, her make-up immaculate. Coldly, enquiringly, she glanced at André.

"André Colbert," Molly introduced him. "One of the workmen who kindly helped me to carry my parcels when I was having difficulty with the gate."

André made his little bow and said *"A votre service, madame!"* Perhaps he hadn't liked being summarily classified as 'one of the workmen'. In rapid French he repeated for Solita's benefit the bit about his father being the works' foreman and that he himself was serving his time as an apprentice. "Learning the business from the bottom to the top," he ended proudly in Enggglish.

"*Ça va, ça va,*" Solita interrupted him impatiently, and said she hoped the workmen wouldn't be too long about the place, especially in her studio, as she was busy preparing for a show. Her manner was off-hand to the point of rudeness. Picking up her cup of coffee, she left the kitchen emanating disapproval.

Feeling deflated, Molly showed André out, her repeated thanks a little warmer than they might have been to make up for Solita's lack of civility. No doubt she was an arrant snob and considered André beneath her notice.

"*A demain, alors!*" he called cheerfully over his shoulder as he disappeared into the lift. "Until tomorrow, then!"

After that it was a race against time to get the cooking under way and the table in the *salle-à-manger* set, potatoes to scrape, beans to slice, the pie to make. Somehow she got through it at last with a few moments left in which to change her frock before Martin arrived. She was still struggling with the back zip of her frock when the door bell rang. She hurried to answer it, the frock still unzipped.

Martin, with his usual air of cool sophistication, stood on the threshold, a cellophane-wrapped sheaf of flowers in his hand.

"Hullo, infant!" he greeted her—the nickname he had coined for her when, young and raw and fresh from school, she had joined the staff of the *Clarion*. "Can you relieve me of this garden produce?" He thrust the flowers into her arms. For one mad moment she thought they might be for herself, then heard Martin say, "I thought Solita might like them."

Flowers for the dinner hostess. Of course! She must

41

be out of her mind to have imagined anything else. Walking before him, leading the way to the salon, she was conscious of her half-zipped frock.

"Allow me," Martin murmured, and with one adroit movement flipped the zip into place.

Molly turned to him, laughing. "Thanks, I hardly had time to get dressed," she said as she showed him into the salon. "I've been running round in circles, trying to get on with the dinner."

"Do you mean you have been pressed into helping in the kitchen?" he asked rather sharply. But before she had time to explain the situation Solita appeared. There was an instant's dramatic silence while she halted on the salon's threshold, then she advanced—making an entrance. In the dimly lit room with its heavy hanging she seemed ethereal as a white flame. She was wearing a cream-coloured caftan of some filmy material, lightly embroidered in gold. It made her look very tall and willowy. Long gold ear-rings swung from her ears, there was a gold chain hung with a heavy gold ornament about her neck, gold sandals on her feet. The effect, with her slanting green eyes, was, strikingly oriental. Molly had never seen her look more lovely.

"Martin, honey!" she whispered, soft as a caress. "Is it really you? I just can't believe it!" She was moving towards him as she spoke, her hands outstretched, and the tallness was suddenly illusion. Martin seemed to tower over her, as he took her in his arms.

CHAPTER THREE

MOLLY stood motionless, amazed at the pain which tore at her heart. So this was the sort of friendship Martin had with Solita Gerard! Why had he implied that he scarcely knew her? Why had he not contacted her when he realised she was in Paris? There seemed to be no answer to these puzzling questions. And there was his odd reluctance to telephone her the other day, the elaborate ruse he had employed, using Molly herself as an intermediary.

They were kissing one another now, with a warmth which was far from the casual salute of mere acquaintances.

Molly fled, her emotions in a turmoil, shattered not only by the revelation of Martin's relationship with Solita but by her own reaction to it. The 'youthful infatuation' she had had for him in the *Clarion* days was still there, nor could it strictly be described any longer as an infatuation. There was something much more to it than that. She found herself in the *salle-à-manger* where the drinks trolley stood ready, and stared numbly at the array of bottles. "Bring the aperitifs in as soon as Mr Varney arrives," Solita had ordered.

So she was to be parlourmaid as well as cook, Molly thought bitterly, as she pushed the trolley through into the salon, where Solita and Martin were sitting side by side on the red velvet couch. Martin jumped to his feet to relieve her of the trolley.

"Will you put my lovely flowers in water, Molly," Solita was demanding in a 'little girl' voice, not bothering to add 'please'. Picking up the cellophane sheath,

43

Molly hurried from the room. In the kitchen she dealt with the flowers, her fingers not quite steady. Gladioli, delphiniums, two dozen exquisite red roses; Martin must have paid the earth for them. The gladioli and delphiniums would make the dining room look a little less drab. The roses she took into the salon, Martin once more leaping to his feet as she entered. She'd have to point out to him that you didn't stand up politely every time a parlourmaid came into the room. As she turned to leave, he said, "Aren't you going to stay and have a drink with us?"

"Of course she is," Solita broke in hurriedly before Molly had time to reply. Her smile was honey tinged with gall. "Come and sit down, sweetie!"

Sweetie! Molly stared at her. "I've got to see to the roast," she murmured, only longing to escape.

"The roast can look after itself," Solita insisted. Rising from the couch, she stood over the trolley, touching bottles with light fingertips, as though she was playing a tune on them. "What will you-all have?" she asked, assuming a soft Southern American drawl. "Martin, a Scotch? I've some of your favourite bourbon."

Molly subsided on to a low chair beside the occasional table on which she had placed the roses. They smelled of high summer and gardens in hot sunshine.

"And what for the child?" Solita was asking. "Scotch, too, or something a little less lethal?"

"Sherry, please," Molly said. And why this 'child' routine? She was twenty-three and had been earning her living since she was eighteen. Somehow it was different when Martin called her 'infant'.

There were various nuts and cheese tit-bits to go with the drinks, a bowl of ice-cubes, olives and tiny pale onions impaled on cocktail sticks. Solita, who had seen to the preparation of the trolley herself, had gone to a good deal of trouble to make it attractive. And she had taken even more pains over her appearance—that filmy, romantic caftan, the long dark eyelashes—surely artificial—the new hair-do. Clearly, Martin was meant to be impressed.

"Incidentally," she said to Molly as she seated herself once more by Martin's side, "you can hold the dinner back a while. We don't want to be hurried over our drinks, and I want to show Martin my paintings before we eat."

Martin said in a puzzled tone, "Do you mean that Molly is actually cooking the meal tonight? Have you had some kind of domestic upheaval ... lost your *femme de ménage*, or whatever? If so you ought to have put me off."

Solita put a hand on his knee. "As if I would, honey! As a matter of fact my cook did walk out today, but it doesn't matter. We're all organised again. I have a morning woman who can see to the lunch, and Molly will do the evening meal."

Martin's eyebrows shot up. "I understood she was here simply as your companion, a sympathetic presence ..."

"But that wouldn't be nearly enough to keep me occupied," Molly put in quickly. Martin mustn't think she had been tricked into the cooking job ... as indeed in a way she had. "I'm only too happy to step into the breach for the short time I'm here. I like cooking and will enjoy it."

"Of course she will," Solita settled it firmly, and changed the subject. "How's your bourbon, Martin? Will you have some more ice?"

"No, thanks, it's fine." He raised his glass to her with a touch of ceremony. "Here's to our reunion, 'Lita, and to your show at the Fontaine."

The conversation, having arrived at Solita's paintings, stayed there. It was all very technical and Molly, finishing her drink, was on edge to get back to the kitchen. She had already started the vegetables cooking and if she didn't do something about it they would be ruined. If only she had some idea at what hour they would be eating! A forlorn hope. She had yet to come to terms with the movable feasts of bohemian circles. Dinner could be at any time between eight o'clock and midnight, and you never knew which. Tonight it was close on ten when they finally sat down, by which time vast quantities of bourbon had been consumed and the studio visited.

Worried over the fate of her apple pie, Molly had blinked in bewilderment at the outsize canvases. Martin seemed to think they were good. Molly found them frightening. Larger than life pictures, some of them must have been eight foot square depicting ordinary modern bathrooms and kitchens, realistically presented in flat bright colours, almost like the illustrations in a glossy woman's magazine, the only difference being that in each of Solita's bathrooms or kitchens horror erupted. Instead of a housewife standing by the immaculate kitchen table there was a witch with black elf-locks, her clawlike hands dripping with blood, her withered lips drawn back to reveal one blackened tooth in a hideous grin. In the bathroom a monster with two heads and a scaly body grimaced at himself in the wall mirror, while in yet another bathroom an obese elderly citizen was busy cutting his throat instead of shaving, blood pouring from the wound.

"Suburban life in the seventies," Solita murmured.

"What's the message?" Martin asked. "The crack-up of contemporary civilisation?"

Solita shrugged. "You can make the message anything you like. They were fun to paint." Winding her arm familiarly through Martin's, she led him from canvas to canvas. It was a vast studio, expensively fitted

46

up and surprisingly spick and span. If Solita with an artist's carelessness ignored dust and muddle in the rest of the apartment she maintained order here. And it was clear that she was an indefatigable worker. The paintings stacked face inward to the wall were innumerable, and as she turned them one by one for Martin's examination Molly slipped away to save what she could of the hopelessly delayed meal.

When they came to eat it the *gigot* of lamb was inevitably overcooked, the vegetables soggy; only the apple pie with its accompanying bowl of Normandy cream could be rated a success, Martin made flattering remarks about it, including indeed the whole meal in his, "I didn't know you were such an accomplished cook, Molly bawn!"

Her second nickname. Fancy him remembering it!

And Solita didn't like it. "I hate to carp," she said, "but the *gigot* was overdone. In France one always *under*-cooks meat, and it would have been improved with a clove of garlic."

Garlic! Molly remembered with a stab. How could she have forgotten it? In France it was garlic with everything, like chips with everything in England.

"Personally," Martin came to her rescue, "I like my meat *au nature*, without garlic or too much seasoning of any kind." He gave Molly his crooked, heart-warming smile. "And I like cooks who have lots of evenings off." He turned to Solita. "Did you know I'd promised myself the pleasure of showing Molly the sights of Paris? Introduce her to a spot of night life..."

Solita's pretty mouth hardened. "Of course, Molly must have reasonable time off. I'm not a slavedriver. But I do work hard," she added pathetically, "and I have to eat."

"So Molly's evening chores are a must?" Martin pursued it, his mouth now as hard as Solita's. Electric currents snapped in the air. Were they disagreeing over her domestic status, or something more personal? Molly wondered. All the evening, beneath their surface displays of affection for one another, undertones of antagonism had lurked—a love-hate relationship. Molly seized on the psychological cliché, but it brought little comfort. Love-hate indicated a passionate involvement...

"There will be evenings when I have engagements and Molly can do as she likes," Solita conceded. With a suddenly melting smile she laid her long elegant fingers on Martin's arm. "Don't worry, honey. I'll arrange for you to show your little English girl the night spots when I can spare her." The artificial eyelashes flapped. "And what about me? Don't I rate an evening or two on the Champs-Elysées?"

"But of course." Martin's smile was enigmatic. "Any time. Just name the day ... or rather the night."

It was almost midnight by the time they had finished coffee and liqueurs and he stood up to leave. It was then Molly was introduced to routine of the keys—which were, if she had known it, to play such a large part in her affairs.

"Will you go down with Martin and unlock the main gate?" Solita asked her. "And be careful to lock it again when he's gone. You'll find three keys on the sideboard in the *salle-à-manger*; two on one ring, and one alone. They all unlock the street entrance."

"Why keys in this day and age?" Martin wanted to know, when Molly returned with the single, mammoth key in her hand. "And what a size! Positively mediaeval. Haven't you got the usual press-button arrangement which controls most of the portals of Paris?"

"It wouldn't do for us here," Solita told him. "We have to be burglar-proof because of our wealthy neighbours across the courtyard. If that street gateway were left unlocked overnight we should never hear the end of it from the *concierge*. We have a Government big-wig in one of the two houses..."

"And somebody might want to take a pot shot at him?" Martin suggested.

Solita laughed. "You never know. But the diamonds of Madame Delormé in the other house would be a much more likely target. Her jewellery is fabulous and she's reported to be one of the best dressed women in Paris."

"Nonsense," Martin said, stooping to kiss Solita good-night. "The best dressed woman in Paris is right here, wearing the most seductive caftan."

Solita's soft little spurt of laughter this time was like the purring of a well fed cat. "Honey, you're adorable!" She stroked his cheek with a lingering fingertip. "When am I going to see you again?"

"I'll call you in the morning," he promised non-committally. They kissed a second time, lightly enough. Once more Molly puzzled bleakly over their relationship. It was a pretty seasoned one, she felt. Whatever interruption it had suffered they had slipped back into it easily enough tonight.

Going down in the tiny lift Martin was very near. He put a casual arm about her shoulder. "Bear up, infant," he counselled unexpectedly. "Solita may have her prickles, but she has her good points as well. Just don't let her impose on you. You've got to learn how to handle her. All geniuses are uncomfortable to live with at times."

A genius. So that's what he thought of Solita!

They had to struggle with the lock of the big gate, which was stiff, and then Martin was gone. Locking up carefully as she had been told, Molly returned to the lift, where the scent of Martin's last cigar lingered. Closing her eyes as she floated upwards, she was sud-

49

denly unbearably weary—in body and soul. It hadn't
been easy this evening, watching Martin and Solita
picking up those mysterious threads. Several times she
had tried to slip away and leave them alone, but invariably Solita had called her back. It was almost as if
she didn't want to be alone with Martin, which was
odd. Or perhaps it was that she enjoyed at this stage
in their reunion having an audience. But whatever it
was it hadn't been much fun for Molly, almost completely excluded from the conversation, which was
mostly about mutual friends in New York. But there
had also been occasional cryptic allusions of a more
intimate kind, when their glances had held, and their
silence was eloquent. Just what was it all about?

Pondering over it, Molly went to bed—having been
bidden to leave all the 'clutter' for Madame Garcia to
see to in the morning.

Letting herself be attracted by Martin Varney had
always been foolish. Now it was sheer madness. Watching his emotional encounters with Solita would be torture. If only she knew just what was between them!
Something pretty vital. There had scarcely been a
moment this evening when they had not been striking
sparks off one another. There had never been any
sparks in her own mild friendship with him. And if she
didn't want to get hurt now she must just get hold of
herself, be thankful for his easy kindness and ask for
nothing more.

With which formidable resolution she wiped away a
shaming teardrop and fell asleep.

The next morning was so sunny and inviting that
it was impossible to go on feeling downcast. Dodging
painters at the window—including young André, who
she had decided it might be wiser to avoid, she went
out on to the bright noisy boulevards soon after nine.
The river drew her. Walking down the left bank she

passed the covered bookstalls which presently would open to display their motley collection of secondhand books and faded prints. Soon she came to the Cathedral of Notre Dame, rising like the prow of a great ship on its island in mid-stream. Crossing the river, she entered by its great west front and spent a timeless interval gazing at its wonders of statuary, architecture and stained glass. Its darkness after the brilliant sunlight was restful, organ music dreamed softly from some hidden loft. When she emerged once more into the everyday world feeling exalted and a little dazed the thought of returning to lunch with Solita was not appealing. She would eat al fresco in the Tuileries Gardens, she decided, at one of the open-air cafés she had noticed there.

Pleasantly tired after her long riverside walk and her sightseeing, she was glad to sit down at one of the little iron tables set out under the chestnut trees. She ordered a big crusty ham sandwich, and then had a strawberry ice cream, with real strawberries in it. Her drink was pure golden apricot juice, lightly chilled. Fat pigeons begged for crumbs at her feet. She bought a soft roll especially to scatter for them. Many other people, taking advantage of the perfect day, were lunching around her; mothers with small children, lonely elderly women, lovers holding hands.

Afterwards she went to the nearby Guignol—the outdoor puppet theatre which is the French version of an English Punch and Judy show, although the characters differ and are more varied. In the open-sided theatre children sat on backless forms breathlessly following the adventures of the cleverly manipulated puppets. Watching their antics—and the rapt faces of the children— Molly forgot all about time and presently realised with a start that it was almost four o'clock. Solita would be waiting for her afternoon coffee.

She had to run most of the way back to the apartment, and as she let herself in at the hall door Solita appeared at the studio end of the long corridor, a paintbrush in her hand.

"Where the hell have you been?" she demanded angrily.

Molly, taken aback by this ill-tempered greeting, murmured uncomfortably that she had had lunch out.

"So I gathered," Solita snapped. "Was it with Martin again?"

So *that* was the trouble! Molly permitted herself a small superior smile. There was a peculiar and perhaps unworthy satisfaction in the discovery that Solita could be jealous of her humble self.

"No, it wasn't with Martin," she answered smoothly. "I ate alone. It was such a lovely day I decided to have a sandwich in the Tuileries Gardens. Then watching the children at the Guignol I forgot the time. I'm sorry I stayed out so long if you wanted me."

"I didn't," Solita conceded. "Your mornings, as I've told you, are your own. But next time you're going to be out for lunch please tell Madame Garcia.

"Did you go out with Martin very much in London?" she asked then, suddenly. It wasn't a very subtle approach, Molly thought.

"Not very often," she admitted. "Mostly it was when he had a spare theatre ticket he didn't know what to do with." An unduly humble reply, perhaps, but it was as much for her own peace of mind as Solita's. There was no use in pretending she had ever meant much in Martin's busy and varied existence. And it pleased Solita.

"*So!*" Solita murmured significantly, and with a mollified air returned to the studio.

"Would you like potatoes baked in their jackets for dinner?" Molly called after her. "They would go well with the cold lamb, and I could get some lettuce ..."

Solita swung round. "We don't eat left-overs in France, my dear. You'll have to brush up your culinary ideas. Get some veal cutlets, perhaps. And we could start with a mushroom omelette."

"But what shall I do with the lamb?" Molly enquired, her thrifty soul disturbed at the thought of it going to waste. "There's quite a bit of it left... and it cost the earth."

"You're telling me!" Solita retorted. "Never buy *gigot* again. It's the most expensive joint of meat in France—on top of which, you ruined it," she ended rudely.

"Because dinner was hours late," Molly defended herself. "And I quite thought you would realise I was going to buy lamb when I spoke of cooking a typical English meal."

"The typical English meal is roast beef," Solita flung back, not without reason. "And for heaven's sake let's be done with this boring discussion about food. I never had to discuss meals with Marie. She seemed to know by instinct just what I wanted to eat."

"Then perhaps you would like to have Marie back," Molly returned, with spirit. "If my cooking, which is about the only thing you really need me for, is a failure, maybe I ought not to be here at all."

"Now, honey, don't take it like that." Solita was all good humour suddenly. "All I'm trying to tell you is that I like French food better than English food. Just you buy what you see in those gorgeous little shops along the Rue de Verneuil... and don't dare to talk about leaving me!" Her smile was warm and dazzling.

These quick changes of mood! They were very disconcerting. But taking advantage of the present one, Molly pointed out she had spent more than the hundred francs she had been given, and waited for the storm to burst. There was, however, no storm.

"Food prices in Paris are hell," Solita groaned. But she went into the studio and producing her handbag gave Molly a further two hundred francs. "Watch it," she couldn't resist warning. "I'm not made of money."

Was she really hard up, or just mean, as Marie had said? If the chance arose she would ask Martin, Molly thought; not putting the question baldly, of course, but repeating to him perhaps Solita's own admission that as a junior member of a wealthy family she was poor. There were degrees of poverty. Solita obviously spent lavishly on clothes, make-up, her painting equipment.

It was all very puzzling. And here I am left with the problem of producing French dishes to which I haven't a clue, Molly mused desperately as she went into the kitchen. André Colbert was sitting on the window sill, noisily stripping paint from the frame.

"Good evening, *mademoiselle*," he greeted Molly. "One hopes one does not derange you with the scraping and so on?"

"Everything is deranging me!" Molly burst out. "I never felt more deranged in my life. Veal cutlets and mushroom omlette. Is there a specially French way of cooking them?"

André gave an understanding nod. *"Ah, c'est entendu!* Mademoiselle practises only the English cuisine, while Madame demands the *cuisine française."*

"Exactly." Molly groped in a cupboard for her shopping bag.

André put down his paint scraper and swung his long legs over the sill into the kitchen. *"Sauter* the veal *cotelettes* in butter," he advised, "and cook them well; this is the one meat which in France we do not serve *sanglant*, you understand. For the omelette; chop the mushrooms and fry them also in the butter before containing them in the omelette, which one fries quickly

54

so that it is just barely set." He lifted fingertips to his lips in the traditional gastronomic gesture.

Molly gazed at him admiringly. "How do you know all this?"

"Me, like many French men, I am interested in the *cuisine*," André explained with some pride. "Also I watch my mother at work. *Attention!*" A look of inspiration came to his pleasant young face. "Tomorrow I will bring you a little book containing some of the everyday recipes she uses : chicken cooked in white wine, the mushrooms eaten raw with a dressing of thick fresh cream and lemon juice, the *boeuf bourgignogne*..."

"Thank you, thank you indeed," Molly broke in. "But please do not trouble. I can buy a French cookery book and find out these things for myself." She couldn't have André lingering in the kitchen helping her with the evening meal when he ought to be on his way home. She couldn't have him in the kitchen in any circumstances...

Looking a little deflated, he murmured, *"Bien, alors,"* and climbed back on to his window sill again.

Thanks to his hints, however, the meal that evening was an unqualified success. Solita actually thanked Molly graciously for the trouble she had taken over it. "I've got to go out," she announced as they were finishing their coffee. "I'm meeting Martin at Fouquet's. I hope you don't mind being left alone."

"Oh, no," Molly assured her. "In fact I think I'll go out too. Just for a little walk. It is such a lovely evening."

"Don't forget to take the keys with you," Solita warned. "I'm taking the single one, you'll have to have the two on one ring. I don't know why I don't have them split up. But somehow I've never bothered. They're a darned nuisance, these great heavy keys..." She went off to the salon to phone for a taxi, and a few minutes later left the apartment, looking radiant, her heart-shaped face alight, her green eyes shining. Molly's own face was not heart-shaped, but comfortably round. Her eyes were an ordinary blue-grey, and boasted no mysterious oriental slant. Nor was she tall and willowy like Solita. But who cared? she asked herself defiantly, as she piled the used dinner dishes in the kitchen for Madame Garcia the next day. At least it was considerate of Solita not to expect her to tackle the disagreeable business of washing up. And where, and what, was Fouquet's? she wondered, as a few minutes later she stepped out on to the Rue de la Marne.

The evening had the warm blue tinge of summer twilight. The sky over the rooftops was beginning to turn pale rose and a spectacular sunset was in progress across the river. Turning her back on it, Molly made her way to the lively Boulevard St Germain where dozens of Parisians were taking the evening air. On either side of the wide road the trees were in full leaf, very fresh and green. Lovers strolled beneath them, many of them picturesquely dressed in surrealist costumes of their own devising, the girls with bright floating hair, the boys shaggy and bearded, many of them carrying guitars.

Reaching the little *place* of St Germain des Prés, Molly found a table on the outside terrace of the famous Deux Magots café and ordered a *café crême*. Across the square the grey bulk of the old church was softened by the flowering trees which surrounded it. The small guide book she carried in her handbag, and now consulted, said it was one of the oldest churches in Paris. Its name, St Germain of the Fields, indicated that it had once stood amid fields and meadows instead of a network of streets, and it reeked of history. Some time she must explore it, but just now she found the people sitting at the tables around her more interesting. The smartly dressed ones would be tourists, the girls with bright hair and the shaggy boys artists or students.

The air was filled with the buzz of friendly chatter. It made her feel a little lonely. In Paris on a beautiful evening in May one ought not to be alone. Molly thought of Solita and Martin, now absorbed in one another's company at Fouquet's, which, she had discovered from her guide book, was a fashionable rendezvous off the Avenue des Champs-Elysées. What would they be doing there ... sitting out on the terrace while the evening sky turned from rose to dark violet and all the lights of Paris came on?

"The Avenue at night," said the guide book, "stretches like a jewelled necklace, sweeping up to the proud Arc de Triomphe which stands at its zenith." A place made for romance and love. Solita at her most beautiful was there at this moment with Martin ...

Wrenching her thoughts away from them, Molly became aware of a distant sound of shouting, which rose above the noise of traffic on the nearby boulevard. No more than faintly disturbing at first, it grew rapidly louder, and suddenly the little *place* beside the café was filled with riot police. Where had they sprung from? Squat broad-shouldered men in black helmets, worn so low over their brows as to give them a faceless, sinister appearance.

The terrace began to clear, as the customers hurried inside the café. Molly realised she ought to follow them, but glued to her seat, she watched in fascination as, batons in hand, the riot police arranged themselves, like giant black beetles, in a line across the entrance to the *place.*

Then, without further warning, all hell was let loose. A crowd of demonstrators running down the boulevard had met the line of police head-on and battle began. Molly could hear the thud of batons, the hoarse cries and screams as students and ordinary pedestrians and police became inextricably mixed. Like some dreadful tide they flowed over the terrace. Too late, Molly made for the door of the café, only to find it bolted and barred. Tables and chairs by this time were flying on the terrace. Molly saw batons come down on unprotected heads. The pandemonium was indescribable. The flailing night-sticks were getting frighteningly near. A young man beside her collapsed, blood streaming from his nose. Police hustled him away, and all the time the crowd by the café door grew thicker. Molly, who could feel her ribs being crushed, cried out in terror.

Somebody was catching hold of her. *"C'est la petite anglaise!"* a horrified voice exclaimed—André Colbert.

"What on earth are you doing out alone in this *bagarre*?" he demanded.

Too breathless to answer him, Molly clung to him, burying her face in his shoulder. Never had a shoulder been more welcome!

The black beetle helmets were now uncomfortably near. "Let's get out of this!" André urged. He had to be rough with her, pushing her through the crowd, until he came to the closed side door of the café. But it too proved to be locked. Fruitlessly he hammered upon it, and as if in answer to his summons it opened a crack, only to reveal a hand holding a small object which was flung in the direction of the police. It went off with a firecracker bang and acrid fumes hung in the air.

In the hubbub that followed André was quick to seize the advantage, hurling himself against the café door before it could be fastened again. Dragging Molly through it beside him, he stood for a moment, gasping for breath. An enormous red-faced waiter almost knocked them over, hurrying to re-bolt the door. Then he turned back, vociferously haranguing a group of young men, demanding which of them had thrown the smoke bomb.

It was nothing, they assured him. A stink bomb; a little home-made toy. *"Une blague."* A joke.

The waiter glared. If it were not that he didn't want the place full of police he would open the door and throw them all out, he declared.

The group dissolved, a little sheepishly, finding seats on the banquette which lined the wall. Though the place was crowded few people were sitting down, preferring to throng the aisles, pressing against the big windows to see what was going on outside.

"Allons!" André said, taking Molly's arm. To her surprise he went over to join the boys on the banquette.

"André!" they greeted him, making room for him on the red velvet seat. In another moment Molly found herself sitting among them, being introduced to a Claude, a Maurice, a Jacques, a Jean-Paul. They were all Sorbonne students, it emerged, and Jean-Paul was André's brother—dark-haired, but just as good-looking in a leaner, more keen-eyed way; a student's alert, sensitive face. Molly liked him.

"What was the demo all about?" André asked, and was answered in a flood of idiomatic French Molly had some difficulty in following. They were, she gathered at last, protesting about the arrest of a teacher they liked in a nearly suburban university. An injustice, they felt, had been done.

"And the demonstration would have passed off quite peacefully," Maurice said, "if the police had not interfered."

"They are always hanging about the streets, looking for trouble," Jean-Paul contributed.

"Throwing smoke bombs at them is not likely to improve their tempers," André pointed out.

The boys looked faintly ashamed. Only Claude

59

laughed, a thickset boy with long hair tumbling almost to his shoulders.

"It was I who threw the bomb!" he boasted. "And I'm only sorry it was so harmless."

"Made out of stinks he pinches from the lab," somebody supplied.

"It's all I can manage," Claude apologised. "One of these days I will do better."

An argument on the pros and cons of violence as a means of protest followed. Once more Molly was lost in the flood of rapidly spoken French.

"You are a friend of André's?" Jean-Paul enquired when the argument had subsided—politely bringing her into the conversation.

"I am staying at an apartment on the Rue de la Marne, where he is at present painting the window frames," Molly explained. "He happened to see me tonight when I was caught in the mob outside here."

"Lucky for you!" Jean-Paul said.

"Yes, indeed," Molly agreed.

"The Rue de la Marne," Claude broke in. He looked Molly up and down with obvious displeasure. "That haunt of the *bourgeoisie* ... it is there I should be throwing my bombs ... among the rich, the mindless, the stupid ones!"

"Molly is not rich," André exclaimed indignantly. "She works for her living, just as I do. Making the *cuisine* for a wealthy American lady, a painter of the *avant-garde*."

"An American!" Claude spat. "No doubt she thinks she owns the world." He went off into a spate of vituperation against the rich, the powerful, the oppressors. It was all a little tiresome, and after a few moments his companions told him unceremoniously to shut up.

Meanwhile the café had begun to take on a more normal aspect. People had returned to their tables and were ordering coffee and drinks. The noise on the street outside had considerably abated, and presently the doors of the place were opened and the evening life of the boulevard began to pick up its usual rhythm. The riot, such as it had been, was over.

"I ought to be getting home," Molly said after her third cup of coffee. An anxious glance at the wall clock had shown her it was close on midnight. André insisted upon accompanying her.

"You must not take Claude too seriously," he told her as they walked under the lamplit trees. "He likes to imagine himself as a red-hot revolutionary ... making his little stink bombs." André shrugged and laughed. "One day he will grow up, one hopes. The others in the group, including my brother, are really trying to think things out ... constructively."

"You mean they imagine they can alter the muddled world of today?" Molly asked a little pityingly.

"Much is wrong with education in France," André answered, "and with many other aspects of modern life as well. My brother and his kind are the new generation. And they are part of a world-wide movement. Students everywhere are on the move, thinking, criticising, rejecting the things which have gone wrong with present-day civilisation. The creation of nuclear weapons, for instance. The fact that five per cent of the world's population owns eighty per cent of the world's wealth, while many starve. In time, much time perhaps, it may be they will be able to right some of these wrongs. If," he ended quietly, "they are single-minded, and their hearts are pure."

Spoken in French this did not sound priggish. Molly found herself liking young André more and more.

"Why did you not go to the university as well as your brother?" she asked.

He shrugged. "Jean-Paul has all the brains. Me—I

61

prefer to work with my hands. And after all, someone has to paint the windows." He smiled down at her. "It is nice painting windows. I find on the other side of them a beautiful girl who makes the *cuisine*!"

They both laughed and when he took Molly's hand she did not draw it away. So hand in hand, like so many other young people on that May evening in Paris, they came to the great door of the barricaded courtyard. There was a brief struggle with the huge key and the stiff lock.

"I could never have managed it on my own," Molly discovered.

"Which means you must never be out alone in the late evenings when the courtyard gates are locked," André was quick to point out. "Won't you let me be your escort? I could take you to La Caverne on the Boul' Mich', an underground club where we dance and sing and have the discothèque. It would amuse you very well, I think."

And why not? Molly asked herself. To be amused very well with this nice André would be better than sitting alone in the apartment, while Solita went off with Martin. She liked André and his quaint English, which he loved to air.

As they parted he lifted her hand and kissed it with a gallantry which only a French boy could have carried off. You couldn't imagine an English teenager achieving it.

When she had locked the great gates she walked through the echoing courtyard to the lift. It was a little eerie letting herself in to the empty apartment, where only the bulging eyes of the Solomon Islanders awaited her. Lying in bed she tried not to think of Solita and Martin still out, enjoying the night life of the gay city. She did not hear them come in.

It was raining when she woke up the following morning, and she did not hurry to get up after her breakfast tray had been disposed of. The workmen, Madame Garcia told her, driven indoors by the weather, were busy painting the insides of the window frames in the *salle-à-manger*.

Solita was unusually affable over lunch. She and Martin had been safely tucked away in an exclusive little *boite-de-nuit* on the Right Bank while the riot had been going on—so they had not seen anything of the trouble. Only that the bridges over the river were closed for some hours," she related. "Which made us very late in getting home."

Silly to feel relieved at this explanation of their prolonged evening. No doubt they had both been enjoying it.

There was a youthful zest about Solita this morning —in spite of her late night. Was it love which gave her this additional glow? She was wearing an unusual white trouser suit of some soft white fabric. The tunic was long, fastened at the neck with a high collar, which gave it an Oriental air. It might have been Chinese or Indian.

"It is a meditation suit," Solita explained when Molly admired it. "A friend brought it to me from Calcutta."

"And are you going to meditate?" Molly asked, smiling.

Solita laughed. "Not exactly. Martin is coming this afternoon to work on an article about my paintings."

Hence the trendy trouser suit, Molly thought bleakly. But she said generously, "I'm sure he'll find the painter as fascinating as the paintings. That suit is terrific on you. Oriental things suit you... that gorgeous caftan you were wearing the other day..."

"I bought it when I was in Tunisia at Easter. It's woven of cobweb-fine threads of ivory and gold, so

63

fragile that it has to be lined with silk to make it wear-able." Pleasure shone in Solita's green eyes. She loved being admired. Lolling back in her chair, toying with her after-lunch coffee, she made Molly think of a purr-ing, cream-fed cat. Life for Solita seemed to be going the way she wanted it at this moment. And obviously Martin had something to do with her contentment.

"What about you and the riot?" she was asking now. "It was pretty bad on the Boulevard St Germain, Madame Garcia says. I hope you were back here from your evening stroll before it started."

"I'm afraid I wasn't," Molly confessed, and launched into an account of her nocturnal adventures.

"So the handsome André came to your rescue," Solita said. "How romantic!" There was a glint of amusement in her green eyes. "Tell me all!" she mocked. "Did he pick you up in his arms and carry you through the whirling batons?"

"More or less," Molly laughed. "Somehow he man-aged to get us into the thronged Deux Magots..."

"That haunt of gaping tourists," Solita sneered. "They must have been scared out of their wits last night."

"I expect they were," Molly agreed. "It was all pretty terrifying. But it wasn't only tourists who were in the Magots, there were lots of students as well, sheltering from the storm..."

"Which they had provoked," Solita added sharply.

"Andre's brother is a student—at the Sorbonne," Molly volunteered. "He was there last night with some of his pals. It was quite interesting listening to their views...most of them as far as I could understand were very sensible, there was only one hothead, who actually makes some kind of childish stink bomb from materials he gets out of the university lab."

"You've got to start somewhere," Solita shrugged.

"This student violence is a menace. I don't know what's the matter with young people today."

Molly tried to tell her, repeating André's tolerant summing up. But she could see she was not making much of an impression. "As far as I could see last night," she ended, "most of the real violence came from the police. It was awful the way they were laying about them indiscriminately with their batons."

"A bunch of thugs," Solita dismissed them. "Special riot police, I believe. It wouldn't be very amusing to get into their clutches just now! You'd better warn your boy-friend to be careful."

"My boy-friend?"

"The charming André, who else? Your little apprentice. And if I'm not mistaken here he is at the window. How I detest these workmen cluttering up the place, peering in at windows! And I thought they'd finished the *salle-à-manger* this morning, the smell of fresh paint is overwhelming . . ."

"*Pardon, madame,*" Andrew called politely from his perch on the catwalk. "Now that the rain has ceased we are anxious to start on the big skylights of the studio. Would this be a convenient time?"

"No, it would not," Solita returned emphatically. "I have a distinguished art critic coming to view my paintings this afternoon. Can't you work somewhere else?"

"But of course, *madame.*" André threw a youthfully embarrassed grin in Molly's direction. Obviously he felt unable to greet her more freely in Solita's daunting presence.

"*Bonjour,* André," Molly called to him. "I hope you got home without any further trouble last night?"

"*Merci bien, mademoiselle.* All was quiet on the boulevards," André replied stiffly.

Solita laughed, as if the little situation presented some comedy which only she could appreciate. "Take him

65

into the kitchen and gave him a drink, or some coffee," she instructed Molly, who felt as if she were being banished below stairs with her follower. But André had already disappeared into the maze of scaffolding which clung to the outside of the high building.

Molly picked up the coffee tray and carried it into the kitchen, where Madame Garcia had just finished the washing up and was putting on her hat ready to depart.

"I'll see to these cups," Molly assured her.

As soon as she had gone André appeared at the window, and without waiting to be invited clambered over the sill and dropped on to the floor. From the pocket of his jeans he produced a small volume. "The little cookery book I promised you," he announced.

Molly, touched by his thoughtfulness for her, thanked him warmly. Then she offered him the cup of coffee Solita had suggested. But he had to get back on the job, he excused himself. "I hope you were none the worse for the fright you got in the riot last night?" he offered.

"Oh, I've quite got over it," Molly assured him. "It was very good of you to come to my rescue."

He bowed. "It is my pleasure to serve you, *mademoiselle*."

"How formal we are!" Molly laughed. "Really, André, if you permit me to call you by your Christian name you must reciprocate and call me by mine, which is Molly."

"Moll . . . ee," he echoed, rolling the word on his tongue with obvious enjoyment. "It is a beautiful name. *Belle, comme toi*," he added in a whisper, and went a deep pink at his own daring. "But for me, I feel I must treat you with great respect, *n'est-ce pas*? You are after all *une femme du monde* . . . of the world artistic. And you are older than I am," he ended unexpectedly.

"Twenty-three," Molly admitted, feeling a bit dashed. "And I am eighteen."

Half a decade difference, Molly worked it out in silence, feeling positively middle-aged. But why the *femme du monde* bit? Was he overawed because she had told him her uncle owned the famous Fontaine Gallery? There was still in France, she had been told, a certain reverence for established artists and their environment. If she was to share in this homage, she supposed it was just as well. If she were going to spend some of her evenings with André a little diffidence on his part might not be amiss. It would save possible complications, keep him from becoming too romantic about her—which he might be inclined to do (in spite of her great age!).

"I'll be your nice old aunt," she told him.

"Now you make fun of me," he said sadly. "Please just be my good friend."

There was something touching about this boy's dignity. "I am proud to be your friend, "Molly told him, and found herself meaning it."

"Will you come to the Caverne with me tonight?" he was quick to press his advantage.

"I'm sorry, André, I'm not free tonight. Some people are coming about seven for drinks and I know that means dinner won't be served until all hours. But I'd like to come some other time."

The door bell pealed. That would be Martin. Molly felt the usual foolish thrill of anticipation as she hurried to answer the summons. But Solita was there before her, looking like a slim Indian boy in her meditation suit. Though there was nothing boyish about the mop of voluptuously curling dark hair, or the piquant face beneath it.

"Martin, honey!" She wreathed her arms about his neck.

67

Over her shoulder, as he stooped to give her the expected kiss, he met Molly's glance and his eyes blazed for an instant, as though in anger. Was he annoyed with her for being there—watching him with Solita in his arms?

But the next moment his "Hullo, infant," was as careless and casual as ever.

Solita turned sharply. "Oh, Molly, there you are! Will you bring us some tea about four o'clock? Martin likes tea better than coffee in the afternoons. Don't you, darling?"

He smiled, and ruffled her hair in a familiar gesture. "So you remembered that?"

"I remember everything," she answered softly, significantly. "There isn't one moment of that wonderful time in New York that I've forgotten." They went off down the long corridor to the studio arm in arm.

Molly filled the hours until tea time writing a long letter to her mother, stressing all the happiest parts of her visit to Paris, not mentioning Solita's difficult temperament. At this time of day her little room was in deep shadow, though sunlight still filled the courtyard beneath. Presently, when the letter was finished, she went over to the window and looked out idly, with the vague idea of seeing how André and the workmen were getting on. But there was no sign of them, they must be working on the other side of the building. Honey-coloured light fell on the façades of the great houses opposite. How attractive they were, with the sweep of marble steps up to their beautifully proportioned doorways, the potted azaleas a colourful splash against the pale sunwashed stone.

As she watched she saw an elegant limousine enter the courtyard and halt before one flight of curving steps. The door above it opened and a tall, fashionably dressed woman appeared. With a conscious grace she slowly descended the steps, while the uniformed young chauffeur, who had leaped from the car, stood by its side, awaiting her, his cap pressed to his breast, his head bent—as though in the presence of royalty. Opening the car door for her, he maintained his almost slavishly respectful stance. Not until she had seated herself did he replace his cap on his head, then scuttling round to his place by the wheel, he drove off. There was something archaic about the little scene. Molly found herself faintly shocked. Servants did not behave in quite that way to their employers in this age of independence. Claude and his pals would have something to say about it, she thought with a twinge of amusement. You couldn't imagine young Claude bowing his head to wealth and position in this fashion. And who was the beautifully dressed woman? she wondered. Madame Delormé of the famous jewellery, or the wife of the Government dignitary?

At four o'clock sharp she carried the tea tray into the studio. Solita in her white trouser suit was standing before one of her largest canvases, holding forth, while Martin, lounging on what looked like a model's throne, listened attentively.

"Ah, tea!" Solita swung round. "Dear Molly! How welcome! But you haven't put a cup for yourself on the tray. Do go and get one."

So she was to be graciously included in the tea-break. Solita was evidently in one of her more charming moods. Or was this an act put on to impress Martin? Molly wondered as she fetched the extra cup and saucer from the kitchen. A suspicion she was instantly ashamed of.

Having invited her to join them, however, Solita consistently ignored her, excluding her from the conversation—which, indeed, soon became a monologue, Solita talking non-stop about the kind of ultra-modern art she despised. "People who put old mowing machines or bicycle wheels on a marble pedestal and label them with a pretentious title. You can say in your article, Martin, that I loathe such empty innovations and consider them puerile...decadent."

When he could get a word in edgeways, Martin abruptly changed the subject by asking Molly when she would be free for the evening out they had promised themselves.

"Oh, don't be tiresome, Martin," Solita broke in before Molly had time to reply. "You know how I hate being pinned down to dates. I've no idea when Molly will be free. It's all so awkward just before my show, with so many people coming and going. Tonight, for instance, Madame Picard will be here for drinks, and some friends from New York who have just flown into Paris..."

"I wasn't talking about tonight," Martin insisted. "Surely Molly has one evening off each week?"

"She has every morning—every day, until four or five o'clock," Solita provided brightly.

"But we can't have an evening out in the morning. What about next Sunday?"

Solita shook her head. "I've invited Molly's uncle to dinner next Sunday, so naturally she will have to be here."

This was the first Molly had heard of an invitation to Great-Uncle Pembury. How odd of Solita not to have mentioned it before. Or was it something she had thought up on the spur of the moment, being deliberately obstructive?

"Anyway, you have competition," she was saying to Martin now, her long green eyes wickedly amused. "Molly has acquired a boy-friend. I guess most of her free time is already booked. Isn't it, my dear?" She turned to Molly with a dazzling smile.

Molly taken aback, went slightly pink.

"A boy-friend?" Martin challenged her, sounding a little put out.

"André Colbert," Solita supplied, once more jumping in before Molly could speak for herself. "A good-looking young workman who's painting the window frames and bothering me to death. But he and Molly get on like a house on fire. She was out with him last night . . ."

"Quite by chance," Molly succeeded in putting in hurriedly, her cheeks now flaming. "He came to my rescue at St Germain des Prés when the riot broke out."

"You were caught in that *bagarre*?" Martin exclaimed, horrified.

It was such a lovely evening, Molly explained, that she had gone for a little stroll along the Boulevard St Germain after the dinner things were put away . . . and suddenly she had found herself in the middle of a howling mob.

Martin, who had left his perch on the model's throne to return his tea cup to the tray, stopped by her side and put a hand on her shoulder. "Sweetie, you mustn't, you really mustn't, wander about Paris alone these summer evenings. It's the open season for demonstrations, and the police are in an ugly mood. Promise me you'll be more careful in future. At least, if you must go out, stick to the Right Bank, which is less likely to be disturbed."

"Don't worry, Martin," Solita interrupted, with a rather annoyed little laugh. "André will look after her. Won't he, Molly?"

"I've no idea," Molly said coldly. Anger choked her. Really, Solita was impossible; ready, it seemed, to go to any lengths to prevent Martin from becoming involved with his obscure little London friend. It was almost too obvious. Couldn't Martin see through it all? He was looking at her now in a baffled sort of way.

"As long as *somebody* is looking after you . . ." he began.

"I can look after myself, thank you both very much," Molly declared, and picking up the tea tray hurried from the studio.

By the time she came back from her afternoon shopping on the Rue de Verneuil Martin had gone and Solita was lying on the couch in the salon looking gracefully exhausted.

"Will you fix the drinks trolley for me?" she called out to Molly. "My guests will be here any minute now. You'll like them," she added with a touch of graciousness. "Madame Picard is the widow of the famous Post-Impressionist painter, Raoul Picard. I'm sure you must know his work—he's the man who did those marvellous dreamy landscapes, and the still life studies, like mediaeval tapestries."

Molly did know them. Reproductions of Raoul Picard's paintings were world-wide and popular, and she was duly impressed at the prospect of meeting the great man's widow. It was nice of Solita to include her in the party tonight. When she felt like it she *could* be nice, with a brand of charm that was well-nigh irresistible.

Perhaps she was trying to make up now for her almost shameless obstructiveness when Martin was here, Molly thought. "Have you really invited Uncle John to dinner on Sunday?" she asked presently as she wheeled in the drinks trolley.

"Of course I have," Solita replied defensively. "I phoned him as soon as Martin had gone." Then realising how she had given herself away, she burst out laughing.

"You don't want me to go out with Martin, do you?" Molly said quietly.

Solita laughed again. "How perceptive of you, my

72

child!" She patted the red velvet upholstery of the settee. "Come and sit down, a moment. I think it's time you and I had a little chat."

Ignoring the invitation, Molly remained standing. And after a brief pause Solita went on: "If I'm being obstructive, it's for your own good. Martin doesn't realise how attractive he can be to women, and I don't want you to be hurt."

"Nice of you to bother about me," Molly said dryly. "But I assure you I can take care of myself. And it seems to me," she added daringly, "that the one who really finds him irresistible is yourself."

"Of course I find him irresistible," Solita returned impassively. "I've every right to. If you must know, Martin and I were more than just friends in New York. In fact we were on the point of getting married when I suddenly changed my mind. Poor Martin, he's never quite got over it. But Fate has brought us together again and we're the best of friends once more." Her green eyes were dreamy. "So it is all set fair for the future, it would seem!" she whispered on a breath as soft as a contented sigh.

CHAPTER FOUR

THE meal Molly had planned for that evening would keep if the aperitif guests stayed on late. And if Solita, as she so often did, asked them to stay on to dinner there would be enough to go round. Molly was learning to cope with these domestic eventualities. Tonight the main dish was a chicken casserole which could be reheated in the oven at the last minute. There were cold meats and patés to start with, and a fairly elaborate salad to follow the chicken. Molly had found the recipe in André's little cookery book. Luckily, people in France didn't seem to bother much over desserts, contenting themselves with fresh fruit. For this evening Molly had bought ripe scarlet cherries and big luscious peaches. They looked beautiful heaped in a blue Quimper bowl.

Surveying them with dull eyes, she struggled with the shock of Solita's revelation. Martin wasn't just casually involved with her, he had wanted to marry her, and Solita had ditched him. It didn't seem possible. Yet it had happened. Molly remembered the mixture of eagerness and reluctance with which he had spoken of Solita the day he had taken her to lunch at the Mirabeau. What a bonus it had been for him, finding that she, Molly, was in Paris, actually living with Solita—the ideal intermediary. No wonder he had been pleased to see her!

The hot pain swelled in Molly's heart. Martin and Solita. Solita and Martin. Not just romantically interested in one another, but ready to be husband and wife. For that, surely, was what Solita's last whispered words had implied. And of course Solita was right. Martin

74

wasn't made of the stuff of rejected lovers. Nor would any woman in her right mind finally reject him. It was in one of her see-saw moods that Solita had wrecked their New York marriage plans—a flash of temperament she had no doubt regretted. But she would make up to him for it now, loving him confidently, possessively, skilfully handling him, bending him just the way she wanted him to go. Clever, beautiful, experienced Solita!

While I'm on the outside, looking in, Molly thought bitterly. That's my place for keeps and I'd better get used to it. Not, she assured herself, that she had ever imagined anything else. But hope was something you couldn't altogether control . . . and there were times when Martin was so sweet to her.

It was a little late for Solita to worry about the chances of her being hurt!

Madame Picard was the first of the evening's guests to arrive, a small, plump old lady with a kindly smile and extraordinarily bright blue eyes. She was dressed in a shabby coat and skirt which she had cheered up by adding several vividly coloured scarves and an assortment of bead necklaces.

She was quickly followed by Vince and Anthea Radwell, two newlyweds from New York who were spending part of their prolonged honeymoon in Paris. They all stayed for dinner, as Molly had foreseen, and the conversation was exclusively of Solita's forthcoming exhibition—the Vernissage, as Molly learned to call it. The menu was a success.

So was the meal she produced on Sunday evening when Great-Uncle John Pembury came to dine. Though he was one of the most shrewd art dealers in Paris he gave an impression of innocent old age, with his shock of white hair, blue eyes and cherubic smile. And it was impossible to be long in his company without being aware of the rare understanding and kindliness which lay beneath his shrewdness.

It took him some time to realise that Molly was doing all the waiting at the table, and when he discovered she had replaced Maria, the household cook, he was clearly annoyed. "That," he pronounced with displeasure, "was hardly the engagement I had in mind when I suggested to you, Solita, that my great-niece should come and keep you company for a few weeks. Nor is it strictly legal. What about her working permit?"

"Oh, the whole thing is quite informal," Solita said airily.

"Including the salary, I suppose?"

Solita's eyes flashed dangerously, and Molly, becoming increasingly embarrassed by the conversation, hastened to say, "It's quite all right, Uncle John. I enjoy doing the evening cooking."

"In fact she offered to do it," Solita fibbed shamelessly. "Positively insisted." She threw out her hands as if to say, "What could I do in the circumstances?"

Uncle John gave a slightly pacified growl. "Oh, well, as long as everyone is happy ..." He turned to Molly. "I hope you aren't hard at it *every* evening. I want to take you about a bit when the Fontaine show is over."

"But *any* time, dear John!" Solita purred. "Molly is perfectly free to come and go as she pleases."

Molly could scarcely believe her ears. After all the difficulties which had been made about her proposed expedition with Martin! Really, Solita had a nerve!

Changing the conversation, she was now busy telling Uncle John that one of the most eminent London art critics was giving her show a preliminary write-up. "Martin Varney ... I expect you've heard of him."

"Yes, indeed," Uncle John agreed with interest. He knew young Varney well, and thought highly of his abilities.

"I used to work with him on the *Clarion*," Molly contributed, determined not to be left out of the conversation this time, nor of Martin Varney's circle of acquaintances.

"Indeed?" Uncle John's keen blue eyes glanced at her speculatively. "You will enjoy meeting him again in Paris, for I presume you have already done so." And without waiting for an affirmation, he added with a chuckle, "I can see I shall have competition in claiming you on your evenings out!"

Solita, never happy when she wasn't the centre of attention, and not at all liking the turn the conversation had taken, began to relay some of the studio gossip Madame Picard had given her the night before. Uncle John swallowed the bait and for a while the talk was all of the doings of the various artistic notabilities in and around the Latin Quarter. Then, deliberately bringing Molly back into the circle, Uncle John asked her how much she had seen of Paris since her arrival. She told him of her walks in the Tuileries, her visit to Notre Dame, and spoke of her delight in the ever-changing magic of the great river with its many beautiful bridges. "I'd love to explore it some time in one of those gay little white steamers," she said.

"So you shall, my dear," Uncle John boomed genially. "If I can't make the time to take you myself I'll find you a suitable escort. I'm a bit old nowadays for draughty boat trips on the Seine!"

There was the usual ritual of the keys when Uncle John finally departed. Going down in the tiny lift which seemed made for intimacies, he asked Molly if she was really enjoying her stay with Solita. "Don't let her put upon you," he warned, as Martin had warned before him. "Like most beautiful women she is inclined to be selfish and spoiled."

"Also," Molly found herself adding unexpectedly,

77

"she is mean. Or at any rate she worries a lot about what I spend for the housekeeping. Is she poor, Uncle John?"

He shook his head. "No, my dear, just as you said, a bit too careful... in fact mean. But rich people, I've discovered, often are. Only the poor can afford to be generous."

During the next three days Solita was busy superintending the hanging of her paintings at the Fontaine Gallery in preparation for her show. Taking advantage of her absence, Molly decided to catch up on her sightseeing and 'do' the Louvre. With Solita out of the way Madame Garcia was glad to produce an early lunch, so on Wednesday about one o'clock, Molly set off with a good four hours before her. She would need them all! There were miles and miles of famous paintings to be looked at. Where did one start? she wondered, as she entered the massive portal off the Rue de Rivoli and found herself at the foot of a wide empty staircase. White, stark, totally without decorative relief, it swept upward, leading the eye to the Winged Victory of Samothrace at the top—headless, without arms, the wings ragged and torn, yet the great statue conveyed the victory its name implied. The mutilated body poised for flight was triumphant, assured. Molly stood gazing up at it entranced. After the roar of the traffic on the Rue de Rivoli outside the silence in this sanctuary of stone was impressive as the winged statue which dominated it.

Peace flooded her heart. The nagging worries of life were muted. Pain, despair, defeat—all these were somehow alleviated by the wounded, dauntless figure upon which she gazed. Even the dull and constant ache that was Martin and Solita... Tears filled her eyes, and it was with a start that she turned when the uniformed attendant approached her. Was Mademoiselle perhaps looking for the Gothic Exhibition? he enquired. She wasn't. But she had noticed the compelling posters outside the building advertising the event, and realised now that it was evidently of some magnitude.

"Where does one find it?" she asked the man. His spate of directions sent her out into the sunshine again, across lawns of scarlet tulips to the south wing of the huge conglomerate of galleries. She passed through a swing door into a foyer filled with chattering women in smart hats. Paying her entrance fee, she went up a flight of steps which led to a series of salons. Studying her catalogue, Molly began conscientiously at Salle Number One. A beautiful Virgin and Child carved in the year 1200 held her attention. A statue of St John had been brought from York Minster, and had an even earlier date than the Virgin. These Gothic treasures, it seemed, had been collected for the occasion from all over Europe. She was privileged, she told herself, to be able to see them. Doggedly she went from gallery to gallery, entranced by the beauty and antiquity of all she saw—treasures from the barbaric ages. Could modern, pinchbeck civilisation produce anything half so satisfying? Only the German crucifixes horrified her, painted wooden figures of a life-sized tortured Christ, brutally realistic.

It was a relief to turn from them to a small glass case containing a reliquary fashioned in gold and precious stones. It represented the Presentation in the Temple, the aged Simeon handing the Christ-Child back to his mother across a tiny altar gleaming with rubies and pearls. It was so delicately made, so expressive of tenderness, the mother's arms held out for the Child; Molly lingered before it wishing she were not alone, that she could share her joy in it with someone who would understand—Martin. If she had come to this exhibition with him there was so much he could

79

have explained to her from his specialised knowledge of art in all its forms. But she mustn't let Martin Varney keep popping into her mind in this way!

The gallery she was in had, she noticed, become curiously empty while she had stood lost in admiration of the reliquary. The visitors, she saw now, had moved in a body to the next gallery which overlooked the river. Crowding about its great windows, people looked out at whatever was going on in the street below. There was a buzz of anxious comment, Molly noticed, as she joined them. Managing to find an unobstructed corner, she looked down at the Pont des Arts and was horrified to find it had been blocked by a formation of police wagons.

"It is the same with all the bridges, I'm told," she heard a woman near her saying to a companion. "I don't suppose we shall be able to get across to the Left Bank for hours."

"It's a student demonstration," another voice supplied. "They were trying to get across to the Right Bank, and this the police will not allow. All the bridges in the city are under close guard and nobody is being permitted to cross them."

With no more heart for Gothic treasures Molly left the building and walked along the *quais*. The sun shone, the boats chugged up and down, the inevitable fishermen cast hopeful lines into the churned-up amber water. There was no sign of students anywhere, but police in plenty, squat, snub-nosed men with their squat, snub-nosed *wagons*.

This, Molly reflected ruefully, was something Solita had warned her against. "Never get caught on the wrong side of the river when the barriers go up!" she had admonished. "If you do I shall be left fending for myself for goodness knows how long. Also I shall worry about you."

I must phone her, Molly thought, and diving down a side street off the Rue de Rivoli found a convenient *tabac*. But there was no reply when she dialled Solita's number. She would still be at the Fontaine, no doubt—on the Left side of the river. Molly tried there and was told by the secretary that Madame Gerard had just left to return to her apartment. She would have to phone again a little later, Molly decided, and recrossing the Rue de Rivoli, walked back to the Tuileries to the Pont des Arts. A policeman glared at her from under his black beetle helmet. Greatly daring, Molly approached him. "*Pardon, m'sieur,*" she began with careful courtesy, "but how long will the bridges be closed?"

"It could be till midnight," he snapped. "Perhaps longer. Who can say?" His broad-shouldered shrug was at once a sneer and a dismissal.

Drifting back the way she had come, Molly gazed unseeingly at the displays of tourist souvenirs under the Rue de Rivoli arcades. What on earth was she going to do with herself until midnight? Go to a cinema? She hadn't brought very much money out with her and the entrance fee and catalogue to the exhibition had used up most of it. Going back to the *tabac*, she treated herself to an expensive cup of tea. Everything this side of the river was twice the price it was on the Left Bank.

Now she was just about penniless. Like a light in the darkness came the thought of Martin. His office was here on the Right Bank, not very far away. Perhaps he would lend her a few francs—enough to buy her a place to sit down in until she could get home across the river. That is if he happened to be in his office. She hoped he was. It would be a comfort to talk to him. Returning to the kiosk at the back of the shop she dialled his number—which she found easily enough in the directory—and there almost at once was Martin's voice on the other end of the line. Her heart lifted.

"I've been caught on the wrong side of the river," she began. But there was no need to go into long explanations with Martin. As a newspaperman he knew all about closed bridges and truculent police.

"It's no evening for you to be out on your own, infant," he warned her. "Where are you phoning from?"

She gave him the address of the *tabac*.

"Stay there until I come and fetch you," he ordered.

Wishing she had enough money for another cup of tea to keep her in countenance, she seated herself at one of the little tables on the pavement outside the *tabac*. It was almost six by this time. Solita would surely be at home now. But Molly was afraid to leave the pavement seat to go and telephone her, in case she missed Martin when he arrived.

It wasn't long before he appeared. Her foolish heart leaped at the sight of him, swinging along the path towards her. He looked so jaunty and sure of himself, the usual lock of hair flopping over his forehead, his eyes wickedly alight as though he laughed inwardly at some private joke.

"Ah, there you are!" he sighted her, and sat down at the little table opposite her. "You've bought it this time, Molly, my love," he said lightly. "Those bridges are going to stay closed for many a long hour. The students are sounding off all over the Boul' Mich' and the St Germain, and Law and Order, armed with a truncheon and plenty of tear-gas, is keeping them at bay."

"I know," Molly agreed. "I actually spoke to a fierce little *flic* at this end of the Pont des Arts and he told me there would be no let-up until midnight, if then."

"And our dear Solita will have to prepare her own evening meal for once," Martin said. Why did he sound so gleeful over it?

"I tried to phone her just now and explain what was

happening to me," Molly went on, "but she wasn't at home."

"She is now," Martin supplied. "I spoke to her just before I left the office, told her I was taking you in tow, and that since you couldn't get back to the apartment this evening I regarded it was a heaven-sent opportunity for us to have that night on the town we promised ourselves."

He held out his hand and she put her own into it, her breath held back.

"Come on, infant, we're going to do things in style. Tea at Fouquet's, dinner on the Place du Tertre on the heights of Montmartre all among the phoney painters. I'll show you Paris by night with its lights ablaze like a hundred thousand jewels, and a young May moon caught in the snow-white domes of the Sacré Coeur."

There was an air of exultation about him. It couldn't be because he was taking her out, Molly decided. He must know perfectly well that Solita would not approve of tea at Fouquet's and dinner on Montmartre for her little household help. It could be that the knowledge amused him. He would tease Solita about it later, make her angry—and then 'kiss her better'. Having lovers' quarrels with the fiery Solita might be staged for the bliss of 'reconciliation' afterwards.

Perhaps she was making it all too complicated, Molly decided, as the taxi Martin had hailed sped towards the Champs-Elysées. The best of men could be obtuse when it came to considering the feelings of their women-folk. Or it could be that he was merely doing his duty towards a one-time colleague. He had promised her an evening of sightseeing and he was keeping his word, Molly summed it up.

"Behold the famous Avenue of the Champs-Elysées!" he declaimed as they got out of the cab, standing outside Fouquet's while he paid the fare, Molly gazed in enchantment up the long tree-lined vista, sweeping away to the Arc de Triomphe. In the late slanting sunshine it seemed a highway paved with gold. Rivers of cars flashed by, their polished surfaces gleaming.

"Noise!" mourned Martin. "Eternal noise. The traffic of Paris has become insane. Let's have tea inside."

They crossed the wide *terrasse* with its beautifully kept trees and tubs of flowers and entered a perfumed interior. Breaths of chocolate and vanilla and freshly brewed coffee hung on the warm air. The decor was lush, all gold-framed mirrors and crimson velvet and potted palms. Egged on by Martin, Molly had chocolate swimming in whipped cream and a pastry so elaborate and delicious that it defied description. Heaven have mercy on her waistline! But the fashionably dressed women around her were all wading into mountainous cakes and creamy éclairs, looking incredibly slim and ethereal as they gorged. Martin stuck to China tea and excused himself for his cowardice. He was saving his appetite for dinner, he said. Newspapermen, he told her, exist on black coffee, which they drink in their office all day long, interspersed with tots of hard liquor when editors became too exigent and the pace of life went mad. "Our stomachs are tanned like a lot of old boots," he expanded inelegantly.

"Spare me the details!" Molly laughed. But he was too thin, she decided. There was the burned-out look about him of the hard-bitten journalist. Attractive— but regrettable. What he needed was a nice comfortable wife to look after him, build him up with nourishing food at regular intervals. She couldn't, she thought sadly, see Solita in the role of comfortable wife.

"What were you doing on the Right Bank this afternoon?" he broke into her reverie.

She told him about the Gothic Exposition, and showed him the illustrated catalogue. He was as knowledgeable about its items as she had known he would be. They sat talking long after the China tea and pastries had been disposed of. But that's how it was in the cafés of Paris. Nobody ever hurried you to leave. You could live your whole life sitting about at café tables if you felt so disposed. Some of the customers at Fouquet's looked as if they did.

She shuddered at the handful of notes Martin handed over for the comparatively minor repast. Then they were out in the sunshine again. They walked up past the Arc de Triomphe and down the Avenue Foch where Martin spied a stray horse-drawn carriage, and declared that they were off for a spin in the nearby Bois de Boulogne.

It should have been idyllic ... the vistas, the green glades, the majestic trees, but even here on the main thoroughfare the noise of traffic bedevilled the air. Martin dismissed the horse carriage and they went down a footpath beneath overhanging branches of lime trees, delicately green and sweetly perfumed. Here at last they found quietness. They chatted easily, Martin full of information about the Bois and the variety of entertainments concealed in its bosky wastes; two race-courses, large lakes, an open-air theatre, a zoological garden. "It would take us a week to explore it all," Martin said, "and tonight we're making for Montmartre. So if you've walked off the effects of your cream buns and hot chocolate, let's find another taxi and make for the heights of the Sacré Coeur."

"Do you think we ought to see if the bridges are open again?" Molly asked rather guiltily.

"Not on your life!" Martin returned with surprising force. "Now I've got you, I'm holding on to you. Bridges or no bridges, I told Solita, this is your evening out!"

They left the taxi on the Place Pigalle and climbed the hundred steps to the terrace of the great church, its white soap-bubble domes lifted against the tender evening sky. From this eminence they could see the immensity of the city spread beneath them, and as they looked down the lights began to come on, like stars falling down into the deepening dusk.

In the tree-filled Place du Tertre they were safe once more from traffic noises. It had once been a hilltop village, Martin said. Now it oozed a sort of arch sophistication, with its whimsically named cafés immortalising Black Cats, Agile Rabbits, Dead Rats and Cows who Laughed—perhaps at the dead rats. At street corners artists in traditional flowing ties and tilted velvet berets had set up their easels and daubed with blissful disregard for any rules but their own wild fantasies. Even the waning light did not daunt them. There were so-called art galleries by the dozen, where gullible tourists trustfully bought their finished work. Side-shows proliferated behind bead curtain doors. Garish posters advertised strip-tease artistes, pop singers, fortune-tellers. There were dance halls, music halls, *boites-de-nuit* by the dozen.

"And once," Martin mourned, "this was the haunt of real painters. In the days of Trilby and Little Billee famous Impressionists came here to dine, and sometimes to paint, when the Moulin Rouge was really a flour mill and Utrillo painted it. Now it might be Brighton West Pier."

But Molly felt she was miles away from Brighton as they sat at a table for two under an acacia tree, eating a superb French meal. It was as dark now as this night in May would ever be and the Place was gay with coloured lamps. A violinist wandered from table to table, playing heart-aching tunes. "Love!" sighed the plaintive melody. *"Parlez-moi d'amour...."*

"How much more corny can you get?" Martin wondered.

"It's not corny to me," Molly told him humbly. "It's Montmartre on a scented night in May, and I'm eating ambrosia and drinking stars."

"Phew!" Martin laughed. "I didn't know you could be so poetical."

"There are lots of things about me you don't know."

He found her hand across the table and his eyes softened, losing for a moment their customary quizzical glint—the eyes of a newspaperman, who knew too much and believed too little.

"Dear Molly, sweet Molly!" he said softly. "You make me feel young again. I wish time could roll backwards and that it was two years ago," he added cryptically.

Before the wounds Solita had inflicted, Molly thought, and gently withdrew her hand from his grasp.

In the taxi, going home round about midnight, he kissed her lightly, tentatively. She pushed him away from her. "Thanks, Martin dear, but you don't *have* to round off the evening with the hackneyed offering of a romantic little kiss. It has been a lovely time . . . don't let's spoil it."

"Spoil it?" He sounded hurt.

"It's just that when I kiss or am kissed I like it to mean something," she explained.

"I see." His tone was dry, even bored. Something had gone from the mood of companionship which had bound them.

Then they were drawing up outside the great wooden gateway of 64b, Rue de la Marne.

"I haven't got the keys!" Molly remembered in panic. "When I left the apartment this afternoon I didn't know I would be out after dark."

"Can't we ring?" Martin suggested. They searched but there was no sign of a bell.

"Let's try knocking." They banged away fruitlessly.

The *concierge* evidently wasn't going to disturb himself answering the summons at this hour of the night.

They retired to the corner *tabac*, luckily still just about open, to consider what they should do. The coffee they felt they had to order was full of dregs and half cold.

"If you could lend me a little money I could go to a hotel," Molly suggested.

"What, at this time of night! Besides, there isn't a respectable hotel handy. You could come to my place. There's a shakedown of sorts in the living room. . . ."

Molly felt herself going stupidly pink. "Imagine what Solita would say to that," she blurted unthinkingly. "She doesn't like me even going out with you . . . what she would say if I were to spend a night in your flat . . . ?"

Martin laughed. "How do you know she doesn't like your going out with me?"

"She's told me so—in words of one syllable."

Martin nodded. "I know. I had some of those words when I phoned her earlier on and informed her that thanks to the closed bridges you and I were about to have our evening out. It seems she feels responsible for your welfare in the wicked city—thinks I might be 'putting ideas' into your head. Am I?"

"Of course not," Molly denied, going even more pink. "And as for being responsible for me—I never heard such nonsense. I'm twenty-three, almost twenty-four, and have at least as much sense as that veteran Solita herself."

"I'm sure you have, infant. But you can be dangerously appealing, you know. I have qualms myself, especially about your wandering around the boulevards with a bunch of wild students . . ."

"I don't," Molly interrupted indignantly. "If you mean my polite little house-painter, André Colbert, he's just a kid, and a very well behaved one." (As for being 'dangerously appealing'; she would tuck that away in her heart and gloat over it at her leisure.) Meanwhile, she finished firmly, "And I wish you wouldn't keep on calling me 'infant'."

"I'm sorry I don't mean to 'diminish' you. It's just that my little nickname for you reminds me of our time on the *Clarion* together. They were happy days..." His sigh was enigmatical.

Madame *la propriétaire* approached their table. "If Monsieur and Madame permit," she announced politely, "we are about to close."

They had better phone Solita before they were thrown out, Martin decided, and leaving Molly to explain their predicament to the proprietress rushed off to the phone box—the obvious solution. Why hadn't they thought of it before? Only that Solita would be furious at being wakened from her first sleep and dragged from her bed to open the troublesome courtyard gate.

A few minutes later they were confronted by a coldly angry Solita in a frilly negligée. Her face was white and set, her green eyes blazing. "The bridges were opened soon after seven," she told them.

"Okay," Martin said. "There's no need to adopt that tone with us. I told you when I phoned this afternoon that I was taking Molly out for the evening." She had never heard him speak so sharply.

Solita, not deigning to answer him, turned and went off into the lift, leaving Molly to follow as best she could.

"I'll go up by the stairs," she offered, feeling more and more uncomfortable. What an ending to their lovely evening! Martin, at least as angry as Solita had been, seemed to be struggling for control. "That woman!" he muttered under his breath. "There are times when I could slap her!"

A lover-like reaction. They would fight about this tomorrow, and then make it up, enjoying the process.

"It will all blow over," Molly said.

"It better had!" Martin growled. "Meanwhile, don't let Solita play you up."

But how to stop her? Molly mused, locking the gate after his departing form.

For the next two days Solita sulked, speaking to Molly only when circumstance forced her to. There were long phone calls for her from Martin and on the second evening she went out with him—so it was all working out as Molly had foreseen. Martin would have explained how casual was his involvement with his little London friend.

Then the day of the Vernissage was upon them, and Solita was suddenly all smiles and good temper once more, discussing with Molly what she should wear. It was to be a formal occasion. 'Evening dress' was printed on the gilt-edged invitation card Molly had had from Uncle John.

But putting on her undistinguished 'best' dinner dress she knew she couldn't hope to compete with Solita, glamorous tonight in black silk velvet, weighed down with barbaric silver ornaments. She looked magnificent, and knew it, her eyes brilliantly alight. This was her hour of triumph, the peak of her career as a painter, and she would make the most of it, queening it over the élite of intellectual and artistic Paris.

With Martin Varney as her escort.

Svelte and assured in immaculate evening rig-out, he stood at her side as she received her guests in the great gallery. Her Prince Regent.

On the skilfully lit walls her canvases were startling splashes of colour against the neutral background. Standing alone and apart, Molly watched the distinguished guests move from canvas to canvas. There were soft-footed waiters bearing trays laden with glasses of champagne and every imaginable delectable cocktail snippet. Uncle John, as host, was impressive and Molly was proud of him, but he was far too busy to have much time to talk to her and she was glad in the end to sit in a corner with old Madame Picard. Now and then some literary or artistic light would drift over to greet the old lady, and discuss the merits of the exhibition : strange pictures of violence in peaceful domestic settings.

"I wonder if my husband would have understood them," Madame Picard mused, in a tone which conveyed that she did not.

"Home life in the Nineteen-Seventies," a well-known sculptor described them with a sardonic shrug, while a haggard young man who looked as if he took drugs dismissed them as, "Schizoid. The work of a genius with a split mind."

A genius with a split mind. The phrase lingered with Molly uncomfortably.

Voices grew louder and louder as the champagne circulated. Witticisms and epigrams, most of them barbed, flew through the air. Dominating the scene, Solita moved from group to group with sinuous grace, her hand for ever possessively on Martin's arm.

"On again, off again," Molly overheard a girl say to her companion, as the couple went by. American by the sound of her voice. "I wonder if it's for keeps this time?"

The companion replied, "It looks that way. I wonder what broke them up in New York. They seemed so devoted to one another."

"It was Solita's well-known temper that wrecked them, I guess," the first voice finished it.

Later there was an interminable dinner at a fashionable haunt on the Champs-Elysées. It went on into the small hours of the morning—a carefully chosen party of friends, selected by Solita from the throng who had filled the gallery. Molly was one of them simply by virtue of her place in Solita's household. She didn't really fit in. There was no tag to her name when introductions were made; she was neither a poet nor a writer nor a painter. So the great ones lost interest in her and she sat silently at the end of the long table, while Solita scintillated at the top.

After an interminable interval they were out once more in the cool night air, hailing taxis, saying gushing goodnights, while Molly looked in horror at the two ragged, shaking creatures propped up against the portals of the restaurant, holding out palsied hands for alms. "Meth drinkers," someone dismissed them, dropping careless coins into the outstretched hands.

"Hasn't it all been too fabulous!" Solita exulted, going home in a cab, her head on Martin's shoulder. When she lifted her radiant face to him, he kissed her. Molly, carefully averting her glance, watched the changing gold and ruby lights as they raced through the city of light and crossed the river.

When they reached the flat she went off to bed, leaving Martin and Solita apparently as fresh as ever, brewing coffee in the kitchen. She didn't hear Martin's departure—he seemed to stay for hours, but she was too tired and discouraged to care. It certainly hadn't been her evening, but to be jealous of the dazzling Solita was useless and humiliating.

Pulling the bedclothes over her head, she was determined to get to sleep. A genius with a split mind—the ominous phrase echoed in her ears. A genius with an almost daemonic beauty, and a magnetism which even Molly herself could feel. How could Martin resist such attraction? It was clear he didn't want to. He was deeply in love.

CHAPTER FIVE

MOLLY woke with a slight headache the next morning. Too much champagne, with indigestible snippets and then that endless meal which went on far, far into the night. Relentlessly at eight o'clock Madame Garcia appeared with the breakfast tray. On the scaffolding beyond the window workmen whistled and sang. The sun shone.

When she had finished her coffee and rolls Molly slipped on her dressing gown and going over to the window, looked out. André's red-gold head was bent over the sill of the salon, which he was industriously painting. As though feeling her eyes on him, he turned, and at the sight of her his young face lit up. *"Bo'jour,* Mollee! *Quel beaux temps!"* He waved a paintbrush at the cloudless sky.

Molly, wishing she had stopped to put a little make-up on her sleep-stained face, agreed that it was a beautiful day.

André slid along the catwalk towards her, walking carefully on slippered feet. Leaning his arms on her window ledge, he surveyed her appreciatively. "You are like a little baby, all rosy with just waking up," he said.

She went a shade more rosy and told him not to be silly. "I must go and get dressed," she said in her most prim voice, and prepared to draw the curtains.

"Wait a little moment!" André begged. "Today it is Friday and we finish the work here. It is desolate for me if I do not see you any more. Will you not come with me to the Caverne tomorrow night? It is very gay

93

there on a Saturday. You would like it." He gazed at her imploringly. Her heart warmed to him. It was nice to be really wanted. Last night she couldn't have mattered less to a single soul in that gallery crowded with Solita's important friends. But it would mean something to André if she went with him to this Caverne place tomorrow evening. And what harm could there be in it? It would be fun. Even if the students did riot ... if there was a police raid. The vague possibilities presented themselves, but recklessly Molly didn't care. Anything was better than being lonely and ignored.

"It will have to be late," she told him. "After I've served the dinner. I'll meet you at the *tabac* on the corner about half past nine."

"Bien!" André beamed. "Tomorrow night at the *tabac* at half past nine. *À bientôt!"* With a wave of his paintbrush he returned to the salon sill.

Drawing the curtains, Molly discovered that her head had stopped aching.

Most of that long sunny day was spent by Solita taking congratulatory telephone calls. Lying on the settee in the salon, clad in her white and gold caftan, she giggled and purred and flirted into the receiver. When it was Martin at the other end she blew kisses. These coy, outdated mannerisms! But somehow she got away with them. Her odd daemonic beauty saved her—she could never appear merely banal.

At lunch time she had the portable phone on the table beside her. When it rang it was Martin once more.

"Martin darling!" Solita cooed. "How lovely to hear you again! Why don't you come on over to lunch— we're just starting." Suddenly her face changed; whatever Martin replied was evidently not to her liking. She pushed the instrument towards Molly's side of the table. "He can't get away from the office at the moment," she said. And then in a flat toneless voice: "He wants a word with you."

Molly picked up the receiver, feeling awkward.

"That you, Molly dear?" Martin's resonant voice greeted her. "Sorry to interrupt your meal, but I've just been having a chat with your Uncle John. He tells me you would like a trip on the Seine in one of the *bateaux-mouches*, and has commissioned me to take you. What about Sunday? Tell Solita it's a Royal Command; an order from Headquarters—or I will. She won't hold out against Uncle John."

After its first leap of joy Molly's heart contracted. She didn't want to be taken out by Martin because Uncle John had 'ordered' it.

"Uncle John is very kind and means well, I'm sure," she said. "But he doesn't have to issue Royal Commands on my behalf. Anyway," she added on a sudden impulse, "I've already fixed a river trip with somebody for Sunday."

"The boy-friend?" Martin's tone was bleak.

"André Colbert," Molly repeated firmly, and was careful to avoid Solita's watchful, sardonic eye.

"Oh, well, as long as you get your trip," Martin was saying. "Maybe I didn't put it very tactfully. I'm sorry, I would have liked to take you...we could have lunched at St Cloud..." He hung up abruptly.

"What did he want?" Solita demanded with singular lack of finesse as Molly replaced the receiver. "I gather he asked you to go on the river. I suppose Uncle John fixed it. He said he would when he was here to dinner the other night."

Molly nodded. "I'm sure he meant to be kind, but I like to pick my own escorts."

"Of course you do," Solita agreed wholeheartedly. "And you prefer young André. Very wise of you." Her long lashes drooped over her eyes. "It wouldn't have

95

been much fun with Martin looking on it as a duty to be fulfilled." She laughed. "Uncle John can be an old tartar at times." After a moment she said, "So I'll have to do without you on Sunday! I like the way you fixed it all without consulting me." She gave Molly a rapier glance. "However," she conceded, "it doesn't matter for this once. I'll get Martin to take me out somewhere. Only don't do this again. I know you must have a certain amount of free time, but naturally I like to be consulted."

She was right, of course, and accepting the rebuke, Molly said she was sorry and would not offend in this way again. She could not very well explain that she had invented the trip on the river, since she couldn't bear the thought of Martin taking her out because he had been ordered to do it. It wasn't so much that she had told an untruth, as that she had anticipated events. She knew André would be only too delighted to take her out for a day on one of the little white steamers.

The next day was Saturday. Molly was just about to dish up a perfectly cooked steak fillet she had prepared, with a special sauce from André's little book, when Solita came into the kitchen looking particularly glamorous in a new evening frock of some clinging blue-green material, that emphasised the colour of her eyes. She was, she announced, going out with Martin. "He's taking me to dinner at Maxim's," she expanded on a note of pride which indicated that Maxim's was somewhere very special indeed.

She might have told me a little earlier, Molly thought, gazing ruefully at the steak which she would now have to eat in solitary state.

"I'm sorry to leave you alone," Solita said with unusual kindliness. "Perhaps you could ring your little boy-friend and ask him to come and keep you company."

"I'm going out with him," Molly confessed unthinkingly, and was instantly annoyed at the glint of satisfaction in the watchful green eyes.

"I'm glad you had already fixed up something," Solita said graciously. "You must make the most of your time in Paris. I suppose you were meeting him after dinner."

Molly nodded. "He's taking me to the Caverne."

The green eyes widened. "That nest of revolutionaries! Be careful, my dear, I don't want you to be caught in any more riots."

"It's simply a place where students congregate to dance and play 'pop'," Molly said, rather nettled. All this exaggerated alarm about revolutionaries! She was sure Solita just liked to make things sensational.

Solita shrugged. "I don't know what Uncle John would think. However, you've fixed it all now, and I wouldn't for the world hinder your love life!" Her laughter held mockery as she turned away.

"Don't forget to take your keys this time," she warned. "And be careful not to lose them. It would never do if some hotheaded student got hold of them." A fantastic suggestion that wasn't even worth answering.

The door bell rang. That would be Martin, and hurrying to meet him, Solita ran down the long corridor, calling his name with joy.

When they had gone, whirring away in the little lift, Molly put the steak into the refrigerator, and made a snack meal for herself from luncheon left-overs. In spite of her meanness about money Solita didn't seem to care how much food was thrown away. But Molly was determined the beautiful steak should not be wasted. She would do it up tomorrow in a casserole, with red wine and tarragon and spices, the way one of the recipes in André's book advised.

Changing her frock a little later she experimented with make-up, putting on a little more than usual. Green eye-shadow was all right, she decided, if not too lavishly applied, but she would never have the courage to wear false lashes. You would have to have the beauty and assurance of a Solita to cope with an inch of extra hair stuck to your eyelids! Anyway, what did it matter? Going out with André Colbert and his teenage pals was hardly a breathtaking event. She smothered the thought of Martin and Solita in their elegant Maxim's, lost in one another, the long evening before them. Would they end up driving in the Bois, the waxing moon above them caught in the tangle of the great towering trees? It was a night for love and moonlight. Walking along a leafy boulevard with André she breathed the perfume of lime blossom and wished she could be away from the noisy traffic and the stench of car exhaust.

"Comme tu es belle!" André whispered, his arm about her shoulders.

"That's not the sort of thing one says to one's old aunt," Molly teased him. He took his arm away from her shoulder, looking so hurt that she was sorry, and was specially nice to him afterwards to make up.

The Caverne when they reached it was hot and crowded, ill-lit to evoke an air of mystery. The decor suggested a dungeon, the wallpaper simulating rough grey stones, on which at intervals iron rings and chains were painted. The dreadful bones of a skull grinned above the well stocked bar. But most of the young people present, Molly noticed, seemed to be drinking coke or fruit juices. Seated on a hard wooden bench behind a rough wooden table, she renewed her acquaintance with Maurice and Jacques, Claude and Jean-Paul. On a small square in the centre of the room dancers gyrated and squirmed to the rhythm of African drumbeats.

"You will that I order the champagne?" André asked her in a tone of awe—a tribute no doubt to what he imagined was her superior sophistication. But having mercy on his pocket she shook her head firmly and said she would have an apricot juice.

Claude, having greeted her as 'our little friend of the *bourgeoisie*', was sounding off as usual, airing his views. Capitalism, he declared, was 'gobbling itself up', the world monetary systems collapsing in confusion. He offered no concrete proof of these dramatic statements and as nobody present really knew very much about the world monetary system, his peroration went unchallenged. "We have got to have fiscal reform!" he shouted above the din of pop music and chatter.

"How will you set about it?" Molly wanted to know.

Claude glared at her.

"Reform of any sort is hard work and mighty slow," André put in. "You have to have a plan of action—not just a lot of talk."

Maurice and Jean-Paul solemnly agreed.

"It would take more than a couple of Claude's stink bombs to settle world economics," Jacques contributed, and they all laughed.

"Anyway, Molly and I have come to dance, not to talk politics," André announced.

Finding a corner on the crowded floor, they set to it. The music was hot and exciting and you didn't need a lot of space in which to work up the rhythm. André was marvellous, Molly discovered, loose-limbed and inventive. They worked themselves up into a blissful trance before they went back to the wooden table.

Later Molly danced with each of the boys in turn. Claude was the least inspiring partner and was soon leading Molly back to the table, where he resumed his tirade against the Establishment. Sometimes he talked sense, but more often it was nonsense.

"Everyone knows," Molly put in wearily at last, "that the modern world has got itself into a bit of a mess with wars and threats of over-population. . . ."

"Sounds like nature striking a balance," Jean-Paul put in.

"Sounds like Governments being darned stupid," Claude fumed. "And we are the generation who have to grow up and somehow try to put it all right."

It was the most poignant argument he had so far offered. There was no answer to it, and for a time they all sat silent, their young faces grave.

Presently three girl students they knew appeared, and Maurice and Jacques and Jean-Paul paired off with them. Molly decided it was time to go home and André stood up beside her, ready to accompany her. Claude, who had been rather left out in the cold after the arrival of the girls, asked if he might come along with them. André, not very enthusiastically, agreed, and the three of them set off.

It was pleasant strolling along the Left Bank boulevards in the warm summer night. Plane trees were brilliantly green in the lamplight, sidewalk cafés spilled over with colour and life. It was some time after midnight, but Paris seemed to have no intention of going to bed.

When they came to the river they looked down at the dark water, dancing with a hundred mirrored reflections. Molly thought of the river trip she might so easily have tomorrow, but the prospect of going with André left her cold. If only Martin had suggested it spontaneously—uninfluenced by Uncle John! But of course that was impossible. She had had her share of sightseeing with him the other night—and that, she concluded, was her lot. He had more than done his duty by his little London friend. Which was just as well. Anything more would have made Solita furious. Why does she bother to be jealous of me? Molly wondered. She has so much!

At the gate of 64b she produced her outsize keys. Claude pounced on them with derisive glee, exclaiming at their weight and bulk. Like the keys of a gaol, he said. "So this is the way the rich lock themselves into their luxurious prisons," he mocked. Opening the gate with a flourish, he ran into the courtyard shouting the old cry of the original French Revolution, 'Death to the aristocrats!'

It was boyish nonsense, of course, but Molly was horrified. Whatever would their distinguished neighbours think if they happened to hear him? He gazed in fascination at the lighted windows of the Delormé mansion, where apparently some kind of party was in progress.

"And in which of these palaces," he demanded, "lives Monsieur le Ministre? *Quelle blague* if one could insert a nice little stink bomb in his august letterbox!"

"Shut up, Claude," André said angrily. "Give Molly back her keys and let us be off."

When she had locked the gates after them she went up to the apartment and was soon in bed. Soon afterwards she heard Martin and Solita come in, and after a short time Martin was leaving, Solita going downstairs with him to let him out of that troublesome gate. Why didn't she give him one of the keys? Molly wondered. Perhaps it was not allowed. They seemed to be very precious, these great iron monsters that nightly secured the safety of the occupants of 64b, Rue de la Marne.

Once more it was a dazzlingly bright morning. As there was no Madame Garcia on a Sunday Molly took a breakfast tray in to Solita. "Why did you have to wake me so early?" she grumbled. "I suppose you're rarin' to get off to that redheaded boy of yours. What time are you meeting him?"

"Ten o'clock," Molly blurted at random. She couldn't unravel her little web of deception at this stage—it was all too complicated. She had committed herself to a long day out, and she might as well take it... enjoy it. She would go on the river alone... study all the points of interest they passed with the help of her guide book.

"Are you lunching out?" she asked Solita.

"No. It's a nuisance, but Martin is on duty. Have you left me anything to eat?"

"There's a beef casserole in the fridge," Molly said, glad now that she had saved that steak fillet and started it cooking last night before she went out. "It will need an hour in the oven..." she began.

"I probably won't bother," Solita broke in. "I can always invite myself to lunch with the Radwells or Madame Picard."

Feeling vaguely guilty, Molly went back to her room and got dressed. By ten o'clock she was walking along the wide tree-lined pavement high above the left bank of the river. On the towpath below the usual hopeful fishermen were patiently busy catching nothing. Dogs released from their leads raced up and down in a frenzy of brief liberty, anxious owners watching over them. Molly was sorry for the dogs of Paris, so many sorts and sizes, dragged on short leads for their daily walks through the traffic-ridden streets. Only on places like the towpath could they run freely.

There was no hurry, she decided, a long day lay ahead of her. Lingering, she examined the books and pictures set out on the bookstalls that lined the riverside walk. Second-rate, second-hand books mostly, and prints and painting reproductions of lamentable hideousness. Though Paris was a world art centre it was also apparently a market for some of the world's monstrosities in so-called art.

Reaching the Ile de la Cité she came to the *quai* where the river steamers were tied up. A tariff of prices nailed to a wall caught her eye. The cost of lunch on one of the larger steamers would, she discovered, be astronomical, far beyond the modest wage she earned working for Solita. She would have to find one of the smaller humbler boats, that served snacks, hot coffee and those great crusty ham sandwiches.

It was as she was mentally totting up the cost of her day out and making sure she could afford it that she heard a voice hailing her. "If it isn't the infant herself, waiting for her cavalier! Don't tell me he's late for his lucky date..."

"Martin!" Her heart turned a violent somersault.

"Are you deciding which boat you'll take when your young man turns up?"

"There isn't any young man," Molly blurted before she could stop herself. "I mean...I said I was going out with André today because I didn't want to be a bother to you."

"Do you know, I suspected something of the sort," Martin laughed. "You aren't a very good liar; not even over the phone."

"Tactful social fibs are not lies," she asserted, indignantly. "I was simply trying to save you a boring assignment. I'm sure Uncle John meant well, but he shouldn't have butted in. I don't like having unwilling escorts pushed at me."

"Spoken like a girl of spirit! The only flaw in the argument is that I'm not an unwilling escort. I'd love to take you on the river today. Cross my heart. What about it?"

Was he just trying to save her feelings, she wondered, redeeming an awkward situation? "Haven't you anything more important to do?" she asked him, and then added, "Solita said you were on duty."

"I can combine duty with pleasure," he declared. "As a matter of fact I'm doing a series of articles on Paris seen through the eyes of a tourist. That's what brings me here this morning. I thought I'd watch the crowd on one of the Sunday steamers. The idea occurred to me when Uncle John suggested this trip. Even without you I could have made something of it. But with you, of course, it will be infinitely more rewarding. We could go downstream to St Cloud. It is a picturesque stretch of river, and St Cloud is beautiful, with nearly a thousand acres of parkland. Ever been there?"

She shook her head, feeling powerless to resist the way things were going. "You mean I'm to be the guinea-pig for your research?" she said a little sadly. "The typical hick tourist."

"Not hick, just tourist," Martin returned equably. "Your fresh eye on the scene will be most inspiring for me, give me a new angle on something which has been written up a hundred times already."

So once again I'm to be made use of, Molly thought bleakly. Yet she couldn't quite suppress the joy she felt at the prospect of a whole day in Martin's company. Her foolish heart seemed to be only too thankful for any crumbs of his companionship that came its way!

And already he was purchasing the tickets. "We won't go on one of those floating restaurants, reeking of cooking, and full of rich Americans feeding their faces. I'm taking you on an ordinary river bus—with a one-way ticket, so that we can stay at St Cloud as long as we like. We can come home by train any time up to midnight..."

The foolish heart soared.

"There's a five-star restaurant at St Cloud. We'll treat ourselves to a slap-up Parisian Sunday *déjeuner* and sleep it off in a deck chair in the park. It's not your English idea of a park," he added as he led her on to the little boat moored to a nearby *quai*. "There are avenues and avenues of trees, miles of solitude ... formal gardens and dancing fountains ... wait until you see those fountains; there's one that rises more than a hundred and thirty feet into the air ..."

He sounded as if he were really enjoying himself. Molly stopped trying to steel her heart against the happiness that was flooding it, and gave him a wide enchanted smile.

He took her hand. "Come on, infant, this is going to be a red-letter day!"

The boat they boarded was smaller than the white *bateaux-mouches* with their above and below deck restaurants. But the seats were comfortable and there was no awning to impede the view. Sitting close to the taffrail, with Martin at her side, Molly could hear the soft rush of the water as the boat cut swathes through its dark green depths. Notre Dame towered above them on its tapering Island. The trees on either bank; as they glided on their way, still held the magic of May in their fresh young foliage. And the sky had never seemed so blue. A morning full of light and movement with the sun giving a glow to the great buildings which lined the banks.

"The Louvre," Martin pointed out unnecessarily. "The Palais Royale. And there's your favourite haunt, les Jardins des Tuileries. Now we're passing beneath the Pont de la Concorde. On your left is Les Invalides ..."

"Must I have my tourist reactions out loud?" Molly teased him.

His hand covered her own. "Just be Molly, my own nice, honest Molly."

She made a grimace. " 'Nice'. 'Honest'. How dull it

sounds!" And what would happen if she were to tell him what this trip with him really meant to her?

"Dull?" Martin was saying. "Did I choose the wrong adjective? Being able to depend upon somebody isn't dull. You say what you mean. You don't have moods and tantrums. It's so...restful." He gave her his crooked smile. "And if that's another ill-chosen adjective, I'm sorry. All I'm saying is that I like to be with you, Molly bawn. You're one of the few people in this feverish city with whom I can be completely at ease."

She tried to look pleased. "That's nice, Martin. I'm glad." But was she? Wouldn't it have been more flattering if he had said she disturbed him, excited him, stimulated him? He makes me sound like some comfortable elder sister, she thought ruefully. Then mentally pulling herself together she reminded herself of her real relationship to him. She was at this moment what she had always been—a girl typist he had chanced upon in the *Clarion* office two years ago.

They were passing the busier *quais* now; long barges with vast loads of sand or gravel or timber raced past them at incredible speed, creating waves upon which their little steamer rocked.

It was noon when they arrived at St Cloud. Molly forgot about being a self-conscious tourist and fell in love with the fabulous park straight away. The fountains and cascades were all that Martin had promised, 'Le Jet Géant' soaring its hundred and thirty feet into the air, spreading out as it fell like a shower of sparkling diamonds. They walked through a maze of tulips and daffodils to the terrace of a café that had once been the pavilion of a Prince Imperial. Here they rested and drank light French aperitifs. The sun was hot and they were pleasantly tired after their long trek through the gardens and wooded alleys.

"Later on when we've had lunch," Martin said, "I'll

take you up the Allée du Chateau which lies behind us, and there we'll find a platform from which there's a magnificent view; all the windings of the Seine, and the rooftops of distant Paris. But for the moment we'll sit here and enjoy this Vermouth Cassis." He lifted his glass to her. "Here's to my girl . . . my staunch one."

She laughed. "The things you've called me today! Honest, dependable . . . and now staunch. You might be composing a reference for a *femme de ménage!*"

"Or a letter of advice to my son, if I had one, on the choosing of a suitable wife."

She gave him a startled glance.

"Lord Chesterfield," he reminded her. "The fourth Earl of that name, politician and statesman of some distinction but chiefly remembered for his admonitory letters to his son."

Molly shook her head. "He doesn't seem to have come up in my schooldays. Perhaps he's a little out of date." And after a pause. "Did the son profit by the advice?"

Martin shrugged. "History doesn't relate. Probably, like most men, he succumbed to the charms of some temperamental beauty who led him the heck of a dance." He fell silent, his brow darkening. Was he thinking of Solita? Comparing us, Molly thought. The dull good girl, and the exciting temperamental one. She swallowed a mouthful of Vermouth Cassis and washed down the lump in her throat. Martin, leaning back in his chair, gazed absently at the vista of trees and flowers. Parisian families on their Sunday outing trooped by in an endless procession.

"If one could only put the clock back!" Martin said softly, as if he were thinking aloud. Then shaking his shoulders, "Come on, infant, drink up. You must be starving. I know I am!"

They ate in the garden of a picturesque inn, their table set beneath a bower of early roses. Conversation was desultory, Martin, like most males when hungry, preferring to concentrate on his food. Delicious food it was too; prawn cocktails, followed by roast duck cooked with peaches, a green salad containing every imaginable ingredient, and ending with sweet little pancakes made at their table and served in a burning liqueur.

"Even the blackest of coffee won't keep me awake after this," Martin declared. They rested in a quiet corner of the garden, Martin unashamedly snoozing, while Molly daydreamed at his side, feeling herself miles away from the Rue de la Marne and the difficult Solita. It's being the loveliest Sunday, she told herself firmly. I'm going to be thankful for it, and not cry for the moon. She stole a glance at the sleeping Martin. Even in sleep he had dignity, though his tousled dark hair made him look like a small boy.

Later they walked to the wooded rise behind the inn and he showed her the view of the Seine, winding for miles through the environs and centre of Paris. It was so clear that they could see the white dome of the Sacré Coeur gleaming on the heights of Montmartre. Pointing it out, Martin said, "That was a jolly good evening we had on the dear old hackneyed Place du Tertre, Molly bawn. You have a way of bringing places and things to life for me."

Words she would treasure to gloat over later, only that she must not forget how lightly they had been spoken. She said, "Solita wasn't particularly pleased about that little outing. Nor," she found herself adding incautiously, "will she like our expedition today. She thinks I've gone on the river with André. Perhaps we'd better leave it like that."

"No," Martin said firmly, "I don't think that's at all a good idea. I'll take you home and deliver you to her, as if our trip was the most natural thing in the world. Which it is."

"You could tell her you took me along as your tourist guinea-pig," Molly suggested, as they made their way down the woodland path.

"No," Martin said once more, "I'm not making any excuses to Solita today. She must learn not to be possessive." He hesitated. "It was that, partly, which broke us up in New York. That... and the fact that she was insisting I should give up my job on the *Clarion*, so that I should be free to follow her hither and thither in her painter's wanderings about the world... living, incidentally, on her income!" He made a grimace of distaste. "Can you imagine me in such a role?"

"Frankly, no," Molly assured him. Her mouth was dry as she said: "You were going to be married... Solita told me..."

"And I let her down. Did she tell you that too?" Martin's tone was bitter.

Molly shook her head. "I understood it was Solita who broke the engagement."

Martin shrugged. "We all have our pride, I suppose. It was I who took the decisive step. Apart from the disagreement about my career I couldn't put up with the endless tantrums and changes of mood, the rows and quarrels which she seemed to enjoy."

"And now you *can* put up with them?" Molly said in a muffled voice, wondering how she was finding the courage to conduct this extraordinary conversation. Why was Martin taking her into his confidence? His story completely altered her concept of Solita's part in the little drama. Now Molly could understand her uncertainty of Martin, her inordinate jealousy of her own humble self.

"Now... I *must* put up with them," Martin answered strangely, "For one thing we've patched up our differences about my job, arrived at a compromise."

Their path now lay beside a small winding stream. It was all very quiet and serene, they seemed to have shaken off the picnicking families.

"After I left New York Solita and I lost sight of each other," Martin was saying. "We didn't communicate and I had no news of her until I came to Paris, when I met some American friends of hers, who told me she had been gravely ill after I left her, and had been for weeks in a nursing home. They implied that it was my fault. You can guess how I felt!" He gazed woodenly ahead of him. "When I discovered she was in Paris I hadn't the courage to approach her—fearful of upsetting her again. She's so sensitive, so highly strung."

"Then," Molly supplied, "I came on the scene. You found that I was staying with Solita..."

"It was all so extraordinary," Martin put in.

"So you invited me to lunch," Molly went on. "To pump me about your beloved..." She couldn't help it if she sounded bitter.

"No, dear, sweet Molly," he put a hand on her shoulder. "It wasn't quite like that. But somehow your presence in her home made a contact. I was invited to dinner." There was a longish pause. "And it went on from there. Certain revelations Solita made to me that evening left me feeling that it was impossible for me to separate myself from her again."

"And now you're both happy once more," Molly rounded it off for him. "I'm very glad." Concentrating on a twig bobbing along on the stream at her side, she fought back the wave of pain that threatened to engulf her.

"Happiness lies at the foot of the rainbow," Martin murmured mysteriously.

"Now I *must*," he had said. Did he mean that he must take Solita's tantrums, her possessiveness? Was he involving himself with her from a sense of duty? But no, Molly decided. That was impossible. She had seen the look on his face when Solita was luring him with her wiles—a corny word, perhaps, but somehow nothing else expressed Solita's way with her lover. She had an irresistible effect on him; a siren's heady charm, and he was powerless under its spell. That was what he had meant when he had said, "Now I must." He would accept Solita as she was; her moods, her beauty, her genius; all the exciting things she had to offer. With his eyes open to her faults he was still deeply in love with her.

They returned to Paris in a hot and dusty train soon after six, although Martin had spoken earlier of extending their day out until midnight. He's had enough of my company, Molly thought sadly. Now he's worried about Solita and is anxious to get back to her. Perhaps he was dreading the inevitable row.

When they reached the wooden gateway Molly suggested that Martin should leave her there. He shook his head, giving her a quizzical glance. "Are you scared of Solita? Don't be. Her bark is worse than her bite, and anyway she has got to learn that even if I am engaged to her I still like to lead my own life, and am not answerable to her for the way I spend every hour of it."

So she was being used to teach Solita a lesson, Molly concluded. That, and the tourist article, just about wrapped up Martin's motives for taking her out today. Or so it seemed to her in the sombre mood that had quenched her earlier delight.

Going up in the narrow lift Martin was very near. "Thanks for the lovely day you've given me," she said, making it sound as heartfelt as she could. She *was* thankful. If only she could stop herself aching for the Martin she couldn't have!

"Was it better than it would have been with your

redheaded friend?" he asked. She thought his smile mocked her. But she answered earnestly and with an emphasis she couldn't control:

"Much, much better. You know it was!"

"Yes, I think I do," he agreed. And then, under his breath he added, "I wish I didn't!"

Just what did he mean? Before she had time to speculate the lift came to a halt and they had reached the hall door of the apartment. As they entered Solita appeared, coming out of the studio in a paint-stained smock. She looked tired and unusually bedraggled—as if she had been working all day.

"Martin!" she exclaimed at the sight of him. She put a quick hand to her hair, as if conscious of its uncombed condition. Wearing no make-up she looked lined, almost old, and no doubt she realised this. It would not improve her temper.

"I've been trying to get you on the phone all afternoon. At your office—at your flat. I thought you might have been free after lunch. . . . Where have you been?"

"On the river with Molly," Martin returned calmly. "We went to St Cloud. I wanted to show her the park and the famous fountains . . ."

For an instant Solita seemed bereft of speech. Then turning on Molly, she said angrily, "You told me you were going out with that workman of yours . . ."

"I changed my mind," Molly faltered.

"It's a long complicated story," Martin laughed.

"You lied to me!" Solita shouted at Molly, ignoring Martin.

"I thought Martin wouldn't want to be bothered with me," Molly offered in some confusion, "so I invented the date with André when Martin phoned me saying Uncle John had ordered him to take me on a *bateau-mouche*."

"She's far too humble," Martin put in. "Underrates

herself. We met purely by chance this morning at the very spot on the *quais* where the steamers take off for St Cloud. You can believe that, or not, as you please."

"I don't believe it!" Solita replied in a voice that trembled with suppressed fury.

"So be it," Martin shrugged. "But please don't let's argue about it. We're hot and thirsty and would like a drink."

"By all means," Solita returned icily, as she led the way into the salon where the drinks trolley, invariably well stocked, awaited. Molly knew better than to follow the lovers. Echoes of the predictable quarrel reached her as she retired to the kitchen for a humble drink of water. Then, either Solita or Martin slammed the salon door, and the sound of the agitated exchange was hushed.

Going to her room, Molly lay on her bed until she heard the hall door close on Martin's retreating footsteps. There was the rattle of the descending lift, then silence. The apartment was filled with it, ominous, threatening. Where was Solita? What was she doing? When would the storm burst?

She had better see about producing some kind of supper, Molly decided when almost half an hour had gone by. Returning to the kitchen, she found cold ham, eggs and mushrooms. She could make an omelette. But suddenly Solita appeared in a blazing rage.

"Now," she began almost gleefully, "perhaps you will be good enough to explain your extraordinary conduct, lying to me, meeting Martin on the sly ... imposing yourself on him for an entire day!"

"It wasn't like that, Solita," Molly offered helplessly.

"Don't bother to tell me any more lies. I know exactly how it was," Solita stormed. "Martin had to do this tourist article about St Cloud for his paper, found you hanging about the *quai*, and you tacked yourself on to him."

Was this really what Martin had told Solita? Molly felt sick with humiliation and disappointment. Though he had said he would not mention the tourist article, he had, in the end when cornered, used it as an excuse. She couldn't believe he had said she 'tacked herself on to him'. That was Solita's addition to the story, but even without that it was bad enough. It didn't occur to Molly that Martin could well have spoken casually of the article he would write about the trip, without having used it as a pretext for taking her along. She was too rattled to work things out.

"You know Martin and I are to be married shortly," Solita's American voice went on at its most rasping. "You know we're in love with one another, but you can't keep out of it. On the strength of some slender association you had ages ago in London you have to keep pushing yourself on my fiancé's attention. You're cheap ... disgusting ... I'm through with you! Today has finished me. You'd better go. Get out!"

Stunned, Molly stared at her. "Do you mean now, this very moment, Solita? You want me to leave right away?"

"I didn't say that," Solita snapped. "Don't take me so literally. Just keep out of my sight until ... until we can make other arrangements," she ended rather vaguely.

"I was going to make an omelette for supper," Molly murmured awkwardly.

"Don't bother. I'll go out to eat. The sight of you makes me sick at the moment!"

With which inelegant pronouncement she turned and flounced off.

There was no point in bothering about supper now. Molly returned to her room to lick her wounds. Solita had dismissed her. That meant she would have to return to London. Without her job here in the apartment she couldn't afford to remain in Paris. She could stay with Uncle John for a day or two, of course, but that would not really solve anything. Without the small salary Solita was paying her she would not even have day-to-day pocket money—and she couldn't start begging from Uncle John.

Subsiding on to her bed once more, she tried to think it all out clearly. Beyond her open window the swallows were swooping and calling to one another, like small black notes of music against the rosy evening sky. Always at this hour they came, and in the early mornings. She would never again hear the plaintive cries of swallows without finding herself back in this attic room, which held for her such poignant associations. The beauty of spring time in Paris . . . and Martin, Martin, Martin!

It was all over now. She would have to go back to the suburban villa that was her home; shut up now that her mother was away. It might be almost a year before she returned from Australia. It would be lonely without her, and the upkeep of the villa, even if it was diminutive, cost something. She would have to get a job quickly. They might take her back at the *Clarion* office, if there still happened to be a vacancy in the typing pool. And if she was working at the *Clarion* there was a chance that she still might catch an occasional glimpse of Martin as he came and went—whatever good that might do her! But she couldn't help thinking about it. Only that he might not be working on at the London office any more. If he married Solita he would very likely get a transfer to New York, or even some kind of roving commission which would allow him to drift from continent to continent at his distinguished artist wife's

115

behest. It was difficult to see Martin in such a subsidiary role. But he had spoken of "a compromise".

It's all wrong for him to marry Solita, she thought, and the pain in her heart was so sharp that it took her breath away.

Getting up off the bed, she washed her hands and face and put on a little fresh make-up to bolster her morale. Even if there was no one to care what you looked like it helped to feel one was looking not altogether drab. It was nearly half past seven. As soon as Solita left the flat she would go out into the kitchen and find herself something to eat. Meanwhile she felt safer hiding in her room. The longer she could keep out of Solita's angry way the better.

The ringing of the phone startled her. Thinking it might be Martin, she waited for Solita to answer it, but nothing happened. The clamour of the bell went on. Putting her head out of her bedroom door, she realised from distant sounds at the end of the corridor that Solita was having a bath, washing off the paint and turpentine before going out to dinner. "For heaven's sakes, Molly, where are you?" her impatient voice cried out. "Can't you hear that blasted phone?"

Hurrying into the salon, Molly picked up the receiver. It was Uncle John. "Oh, that's Molly, is it? Good! I was beginning to be afraid you were both out. Is Solita about?"

"She's having a bath, Uncle John," Molly explained.

"Oh, well, it doesn't matter. You can give her a message. Tell her I have some splendid news for her." He seemed to be overflowing with good cheer. "Those two largest canvases of hers—the ones we thought we would never get off our hands... I've had a splendid offer for them from New York, and for several of the smaller ones as well. In fact most of the works she showed at her Vernissage are now taken care of. Isn't that some-

116

thing to celebrate? I'm coming round to discuss it all with Solita right away. Tell you what!" he ended genially. "I'll take you both out to dinner at the Chateau d'Eau in the Bois de Boulogne. We'll eat in the moonlight under the May blossom, drink to Solita's success in champagne. Run along and tell Solita to put on her prettiest frock and I'll be along to collect you both in half an hour."

As Molly replaced the receiver Solita appeared, wrapped in a towel, at the bathroom door. "Who was it?" she demanded bluntly.

"My Uncle John," Molly said. "He asked me to tell you that he's had a good offer from America for two of your largest canvases, and he's coming round right away to discuss it with you."

Solita's green eyes lit up. "My, isn't that marvellous! My two white elephants finding a home! All the critics, including Martin, thought I was crazy to paint on that scale. But you see how wrong they were?" She cuddled the big bath towel closer around her and positively beamed. All her ill temper seemed to have evaporated.

"It's a little awkward," Molly began hesitatingly, "but Uncle John says he wants to take us both out to dinner. I mean, you won't want me tagging along ... having dismissed me and so on."

Surprisingly, Solita laughed. "And you jolly well deserved to be dismissed," she said cheerfully. "The trouble with you, my poor Molly, is that you have no sense ... no tact. The clumsy way you pursue Martin would be funny if it were not so annoying. But it's silly of me to mind—since your pursuit is so futile; something Martin and I can smile over together. So forget our little quarrel and come along and have dinner with your uncle as he suggests. After all I can't very well sack you under his nose...he wouldn't like it at all, and Uncle John is someone I really can't afford to upset."

At least she's being honest about it, Molly thought keeping me on because Uncle John's good will is vital to her career. Nor was there anything out of the ordinary about her lightning change of mood. Her rages were frightening, but it took very little to make her forget them, when it suited her. And obviously it suited her now.

The restaurant Uncle John took them to in the Bois was a pretty white building half hidden by trees. They ate on a vast, lamplit terrace, opening on to a green lawn; flower beds and shrubs were cunningly floodlit. The laburnum trees looked like golden fountains, their flower-laden branches reaching almost to the grass beneath them. Floodlit banks of azaleas were dramatic; there was a floodlit pond where waterlilies slept.

Eating a delicious meal, listening to Solita and Uncle John talking their mixture of business and studio gossip, Molly felt she was really in Paris. It was moments like this that made her stay memorable. From an educational viewpoint, she added to herself. Her trip to St Cloud earlier in this endless day had other values. The stars in her eyes deepened. For all its ups and downs it had been a pretty marvellous Sunday.

"What is this rumour I hear about a romance between you and young Varney?" Uncle John was asking Solita.

She gave him a languishing glance from under her long lashes. "It's quite true. Martin and I are going to be married."

"Congratulations, my dear!" Uncle John offered with evident approval. "And what does our Molly think of this?" he asked across the table.

Molly, taken by surprise, said a little breathlessly, "I ...add my congratulations, of course." But it wasn't very convincing. Solita flashed her a glance of naked antipathy and triumph.

"What about inviting him to join us?" Uncle John suggested. He glanced at his watch. "You might find him still at his office if he's doing Sunday duty."

"What a marvellous idea," Solita agreed at once. "I'll go and phone him. He *is* on duty—writing some tiresome little article on tourist river trips. But I'm sure he'll be finished by now." Confidence rang in her every word. Apparently she had already forgotten the bitter reproaches with which she had greeted her lover earlier in the evening. Their quarrel, such as it was, had been quickly patched up. Martin's excuses for his day on the river must have been pretty convincing, Molly thought sadly. But why should they not have been? An innocent, almost accidental outing, saving him from the boredom of a hackneyed assignment.

She watched Solita crossing the floodlit lawn, tall and lithe in her brief, sleeveless white frock. Her arms and shoulders were becomingly tanned, her dark hair piled in a Grecian knot on the crown of her head. False curls, Molly guessed, but none the less becoming for that and very *à la mode*. Heads turned to look after her as she crossed the terrace—female as well as male.

"Young Martin must be proud of her," Uncle John murmured, gazing admiringly after her retreating figure —a remark to which Molly felt she could offer no comment.

Presently Solita was back, saying Martin would be with them as soon as he could grab a taxi. And in a miraculously short time, there he was.

"Just in time for coffee," he declared, and, after kissing Solita, he took the empty chair next to Molly. He had already eaten, he explained; a snack supper at a *bistro* near the office. "Anyway I had such a gargantuan lunch at St Cloud today I don't think I could have done the Chateau d'Eau *cuisine* justice." He looked a little tired and dishevelled.

"Did you get your article done?" Solita enquired with almost wifely concern.

"Just about." He turned to give Molly his lopsided smile. "You'll hate it when you read it in tomorrow's edition, as banal as can be."

"Tourist stuff, what can you expect?" Solita put in with obvious scorn for all tourists—including Molly.

"Shamelessly faked," Martin was saying, "since the companion I had with me was anything but a tourist in her responses to the day's experiences. You liked St Cloud, didn't you, Moll?"

Molly nodded agreement. "It was fabulous!" she murmured inadequately, and was unable to add anything more original. No wonder Martin instantly lost interest in her, listening in surprised delight to the wonderful news of Solita's latest picture sale.

"The Rothenstein Gallery in New York ... think of it!" Solita exulted. "Uncle John thinks I ought to go over and see the canvases hung."

"It isn't every day," Uncle John chimed in, "that the work of one of my clients is included in what must be almost the most esoteric collection of modern paintings in the world. I think Solita should undoubtedly put in an appearance. It would be good publicity. Why don't you go along with her?" he added, turning to Martin.

"I don't imagine the *Clarion* would stand for it," Martin answered, a little too quickly. "They've got a good art man in New York already."

"Take a holiday, then. A honeymoon holiday," Uncle John expanded, warmed by the celebratory champagne he had ordered. "A wedding journey and a gallery triumph all in one for our beautiful Solita. What could be better?"

Solita put a slim brown hand on Martin's wrist. "What about it, honey?" Her eyes were soft and pleading.

Martin covered her hand with his own. Looking down at her, his face revealed conflicting emotions. "Don't rush me, sweet. A wedding trip ... that would take a bit of arranging."

"Nonsense!" boomed Uncle John, quite carried away by the romance of the moment. "The less arranging you go in for in these matters, the better. Get a special licence ... pop into the nearest Mairie, and there you are!"

Martin said firmly, "I wouldn't want to be married in France."

"In New York, then," Solita said.

Had she no shame? Molly wondered, no sensitivity ... trying to rush Martin into a marriage date, here in public, so to speak. She could feel the way he was stiffening himself against it, sense his reluctance.

"Shall we discuss it some other time?" he was saying, and his voice was cold.

Solita's face darkened, but she managed one of her coquettish smiles. "Of, course, darling! We mustn't let Uncle John's enthusiasm carry us away. There's a lot to be thought of."

As she drew her hand away from Martin's grasp she shot a glance at Molly. It was quick as the dart of a cobra's tongue—and as deadly.

Because I witnessed her rebuff, Molly thought uneasily. But the moment passed and Uncle John was suggesting they should go on to a new night club which had just opened on the Champs-Elysées.

"You get about, don't you, Uncle John?" Solita laughed.

A wealthy client had taken him there on the night the place opened, Uncle John explained. La Boîte de la

Lune, when they reached it, proved to be small but luxurious. As it was still early in the evening by Paris standards it was not yet full, and the beautifully sprung dance floor was practically empty. A band composed of piano and strings played dreamy old-fashioned dance tunes which evidently wakened echoes in Uncle John's heart. As soon as they had chosen their table he was up and away with Solita in his arms. Watching them, Martin laughed. "The old boy is surprisingly light on his toes. Shall we follow their example, infant?"

They danced for a while in silence, Molly all too conscious of Martin's nearness, hoping he would not feel the hurried beating of her heart—that foolish, uncontrollable organ! The lights dimmed and they moved in a coloured twilight, walking now, rather than dancing. He was holding her very close.

"Was it very bad when I left you this afternoon?" he asked. "Solita's rages can be terrifying, I know."

"It wasn't too bad," Molly assured him, hurriedly assembling her wits. Her afternoon encounter with the angry Solita now seemed aeons away. "Naturally she was a bit upset," she added mildly.

Martin laughed. "Loyal little soul, aren't you? The mood she was in I was half afraid to leave you with her."

"It was all a silly misunderstanding," Molly minimised the affair. "She'd heard me refusing to go on the river with you, and I *had* let her think I was going with André."

"What exactly does this André character mean to you?" Martin demanded abruptly, shelving Solita for the moment.

Molly hesitated. "He's part of my Paris experience, I suppose. It's interesting to meet a real French boy, and it's good for my French, talking to him. He's very charming in a Continental way, but most correct. In fact, *très gentil*."

"And you aren't a little bit in love with him?"

"Good heavens, no! He's years my junior, for one thing...and if he were not it wouldn't make any difference. He's just someone nice and companionable."

Martin said, "I guessed that's how it was, but thought I'd ask. Hope you didn't mind?"

"Not at all," Molly returned a little stiffly. Martin's interest in her love life must not be taken seriously. There was an inquisitive streak in him where people and their relationships were concerned. She had noticed it once or twice before and concluded it was his newspaperman's curiosity.

The dance tune changed and Molly saw that Uncle John and Solita were now sitting down. But Martin showed no sign of releasing her.

"Listen," he said, suddenly, urgently. "This may sound a bit dramatic, but if you ever feel scared of Solita ring me up and I'll come."

Molly lifted wide blue eyes. "Scared?" she echoed incredulously.

"There are times when Solita's rages seem to be uncontrollable. I know how to handle her, but it might be too much for you. It's..." he was speaking now with obvious reluctance, "a legacy from her illness in New York last year, something she'll outgrow, of course. But in the meantime..." the words trailed away inconclusively. "It's something she has discussed with me quite openly, poor kid."

Trading on his compassion. Molly smothered the thought, and the jealousy that had given rise to it. After all, she knew nothing of the nature of Solita's illness. A nervous breakdown, perhaps. Martin had broken her heart at one time, it seemed, and he would have to spend the rest of his life mending it. It was a good thing he was in love with her—perhaps all the more in love because of the wrong he felt he had done to her.

But small irrepressible doubts lingered. You couldn't imagine Solita's heart being really broken. Her pride could be hurt, but not her heart. Molly doubted if she possessed such an organ. But she would never forgive a slight. The Martin who had walked out on her must be brought to heel good and proper!

As soon as they were back at their table, he held out his arms to her and she went to him with her quietly triumphant smile. He might have a duty dance with Molly, but it was for this moment he had been waiting.

Watching them, Uncle John said it was wonderful to see two young people so much in love and so well suited to one another. "Young Varney will be the ideal husband for Solita," the old man pronounced. "An up-and-coming art critic with many valuable contacts. He'll be most useful to her in her career."

A little later when Solita and Martin were once more dancing, he suggested to Molly that they should go home. "I'm a little tired," he said, "and the truth is, my dear Molly, you and I are not really needed here. In fact we're probably in the way."

There were polite protests from Solita and Martin when they made their farewells, but it was clear they were both relieved at Uncle John's suggestion that he should see Molly home.

During the next few days Solita was unusually good-tempered. She was delighted about the sale of her two outsize canvases, and was enjoying the preparations for her journey to New York. Many of the pictures in her Fontaine exhibition had sold well and she was obviously in funds, buying frocks and outfits for her New York visit. Was it in fact a trousseau? Molly couldn't help wondering, seeing the dress boxes frothing over with tissue paper.

Life went smoothly, on the surface at all events.

Martin came and went, seeming to spend all the time he could spare from his newspaper duties with Solita. As neither of them was communicative, Molly was left guessing about their wedding plans. But there was obviously no argument between them. And it seemed equally obvious, as Uncle John had observed, that they were very much in love.

Late one evening, after dinner, André phoned Molly and asked her if she would like to come and have a drink with him at the Deux Magots. Martin and Solita had gone off to some kind of midnight artistic soirée and it was lonely in the flat, so, thankfully, Molly accepted the invitation.

The popular café was as usual crowded. They found seats on the outdoor *terrasse*, opposite the old church, aloof behind its screen of trees, its floodlit tower lifted the eye to the soft night sky ... a wistful reminder of peace and quietness amid the endless clamour of the boulevard traffic. They had to lift their voices to make themselves heard above the scream of the car engines.

Her time in Paris was running out, Molly told André, and saw the shadow in his eyes. "When Solita goes to New York my job will come to an end," she said.

André sat silent a while, his young face set. Then he put his hand on the banquette between them, and Molly, interpreting the gesture, slipped her own into it. His grip was strong and hard, the work-roughened fingers holding hers as if they would never let go. "If I were older ... already a man of affairs, would you stay in Paris with me?" he asked in a choked voice.

"A man of affairs?" Molly echoed.

"That is not the good English ... no? How do you say it, then? The man of success, who establishes himself, makes much money in business?"

Molly laughed. "The sort of man I really couldn't bear! I'd much rather have a boy with long golden lashes, who sings outside my attic window in the early mornings, waving a smelly paintbrush in the air."

"Now you mock me," André said sadly, relinquishing her hand. "But I understand your meaning. I am young, with my fortunes to make. If we had met a few years later ... or if," he added with an apparent callousness due to his awkwardness with English, "you had not been so old ..."

Molly laughed again. "You don't spare my middle-aged feelings, André, but I think I know what you mean. 'It is never the time and the place and the loved one all together,' " she quoted softly, and it was not André's face she was seeing now, but Martin's. And she could hear him saying strangely. "If only it were two years ago ... if time would roll back. ..." A remark he had made that night in Montmartre. That was no doubt completely impersonal, involving no more than his troubled time in New York when, with unhappiness on both sides, he and Solita had temporarily parted.

"In school," André was saying, "we had a Professor of Literature who used to say : 'Life is timing'. I wondered what he meant. Now," he ended wistfully, "I think I know."

When he left her at the gateway of 64b, Rue de la Marne a little later, he kissed her—for the first time, and she knew it was a kiss of farewell. Practical as only a Frenchman can be in such matters, he did not suggest seeing her again.

CHAPTER SIX

NOW it was the last week in May. Walking through the Tuileries the next morning, Molly watched the pink and white chestnut blossoms flutter thickly to the ground. Someone had splashed her favourite group of statuary with red paint—the revolutionary red. On the plinth of the statue the huge word '*Non*' had been scrawled, also in violent red. "No," to everything the established order stood for.

It was a beautiful group, two lovers embracing, a little lamb at their feet. The tenderness of the man leaning over the submissive girl was subtly conveyed—a poem in stone, and the vicious daubings were an insult.

A lump came into Molly's throat as she looked at this evidence of vandalism, bringing the turmoil of those strange spring days into the leafy sanctuary. Out on the boulevards the marchings and counter-marchings were increasing. Police *wagons* abounded, their raucous klaxons shrill above the noise of the traffic, while overhead hovering helicopters kept watch for trouble spots. Tension brooded in the air, but undismayed, the life of Paris went on, the pavement *terrasses* were as crowded as ever with tourists and those mysteriously idle Parisians who seem to have nothing to do all day long but sit in the sun and gossip and drink. It was all very carefree and gay, and the growing hints of revolution were not to be taken seriously.

Was there anywhere else in the world, Molly wondered, where there were so many invitations to sit in the sunshine and dream the hours away? Nor could there be anywhere else where a cup of coffee or a glass of fruit juice could be made to last so long. You could linger on the most fashionable of *terrasses* all morning, or all evening, on the strength of one small item ordered. The waiters never hustled you, never presented bills.

She would miss it all, Molly thought, when she got back to the more prosaic atmosphere of London.

But she must not hurry away, Uncle John persuaded her, when she spoke to him one day of her imminent departure. He would be delighted to have her for a little while in his small flat. "Madame Solange, my very good housekeeper, will look after you," he promised.

"I am going to stay a few days with my uncle when I leave here," Molly told Solita over lunch the same day.

"Indeed!" Solita snapped, clearly displeased. All along it had been plain that she was jealous of Molly's relationship with the eminent gallery-owner. It would have suited her better if her little domestic helper's family connections had been more obscure.

"You're in a great hurry to make your plans," she grumbled. "I haven't yet been able to fix the date of my departure for New York."

Was she waiting for Martin to make up his mind to accompany her? There had been no announcement about an imminent marriage ... Molly couldn't help speculating about it, as she watched them together. It was surely no more than a matter of days before everything would be finally settled. Or so Molly persuaded herself. Somehow it was easier that way. Any doubt of Martin's total involvement roused in her such a storm of emotion that she firmly resisted such doubts.

Then something happened which effectively shattered her precarious peace of mind.

It was on the day she had spoken to Solita of her plan to stay with Uncle John that Martin arrived unexpectedly just after lunch, saying he had two tickets for a rather special matinée at the Odéon Theatre. "A puppet show from the famous Bunraku Puppet Theatre in Tokyo," he explained. "Would you care to see it, Solita?"

"I loathe puppets," Solita declared. "They bore me stiff."

"But this isn't ordinary puppetry," Martin pleaded. "It's a Japanese art form three hundred years old. I'm writing a piece for the *Clarion* about it, and," he glanced around desolately, "I hate going alone. If you don't want to come, Solita, perhaps Molly would take pity on me?"

"If Solita doesn't mind?" Molly offered nervously.

"Why should I mind?" Solita snapped. "And whether I do or not won't bother Martin, I imagine."

Martin, unruffled, put an arm around her shoulder. "You know I 'bother', as you put it, where your happiness is concerned. But this is such a trivial thing. What," he laughed, "is the odd puppet show between friends?"

"What indeed?" Solita agreed, appeased. She lifted his hand and laid it against her cheek. Dreamily she glanced at Molly, standing uncertainly by. "Run along, child, and get ready," she ordered. "If you're going to be in time for that matinée, both of you, you'd better be off."

With her gracious permission, Molly thought bitterly as she went to her room to make what hurried preparations she might . . . for this trip to the theatre which Martin considered too trivial to be worth discussion. Just another newspaperman's assignment, and a spare theatre ticket to be handed to anyone willing to come along.

As she hastily ran a comb through her hair and repaired her make-up she despised herself for the flutter of joyful expectancy which filled her heart. One more afternoon with Martin. One more memory to carry away with her when these Paris days were left behind.

In spite of Solita's admonitions and Molly's haste they were a little late, and the performance had already begun when they reached the theatre. Martin held Molly's hand as they groped their way to their seats—press seats, in a favourable row of the stalls, but sufficiently far back to give the brilliantly lit stage its necessary focus.

For the first few minutes Molly had to repress the desire to giggle. The almost life-sized puppets on the stage were, at a first glance, so grotesque; mouthing, gesturing, wagging their heads, each puppet manipulated by no less than three human actors. Draped from head to foot in black, not even their faces showing, they looked like ghouls. Heightening the bizarre effect, the story the puppets were miming was relayed by a narrator, wailing in shrill Japanese, from a box high above the auditorium on the right-hand side of the stage. The wailing, which at times became a series of shrill squeals, was accompanied by wild notes of music plucked from a samisen, a type of oriental guitar. Comical to begin with, it was amazing how soon the magic of the whole procedure began to work.

The story concerned the suicide of two ill-fated lovers. It was fantastic how the very expressions on their puppet faces appeared to change as their tragic history unfolded. Their gestures were delicate, their movements graceful and precise, formalised, yet completely convincing. And they were, of course, beautifully dressed, with traditional Japanese artistry. The scenery surrounding them, though simple, was all in harmony with the mood of the little drama.

Gradually the human manipulators in the background ceased to matter, or even to exist—one simply did not see them any more. The puppet lovers, taking on a strange life of their own, dominated everything. It was fairly easy to follow what was happening to them. Rather than be parted by a series of circumstances, made plain in the French programme notes, they decided to die together. So far it was a cliché situation. It was the elaborate Japanese ritual which led up to the joint suicide that gave to the play its special significance, and the final scene of tenderness between the two little figures before the end was almost unbearably poignant. Then, as the stage slowly darkened, the lover killed his sweetheart with a sword thrust, and after another sequel of ritual, accompanied by sobs from the guitar, the lover too fell upon his sword in the best Oriental tradition.

Other one-act plays followed, some of them pure comedy, all of them brilliantly put on. But Molly felt it was the first play she would remember. When they came out, late afternoon sunshine flooded the Place de l'Odéon. They walked to the nearby Boulevard St Germain, silent, each absorbed in their own thoughts, still caught in the mood of enchantment which the best in the theatre invariably invokes. The real world did not look quite real, and it only gradually dawned on them that the groups of talking and gesticulating students were even more lively than usual.

Like all true-born journalists, perennially on duty, ears pricked for news, Martin stopped and spoke to one knot of boys. An excited flow of French answered his questions. There had been 'a bit of a demonstration', Molly gathered. Some arrests had been made.

Passing a hand across his eyes, as though waking from a dream to the harsh actualities of life, Martin suggested they should stop at a café and have a drink.

"I ought to get back and see to Solita's evening meal," Molly pointed out.

But Martin led her firmly on to a glass-enclosed

131

terrasse and taking her gently by the shoulder sat her down on a spindly chair, flanked by a small table. "You don't have to worry about Solita's dinner tonight," he said. "I'll take her out.

"Tea or aperitiff?" he enquired, seating himself beside her.

She was dying for a cup of tea, she admitted. "All that emotion and colour and drama in the theatre has given me the exhausted feeling that only tea can relieve."

Martin took the programme from his pocket and looking at it over his shoulder, Molly read once again, and more thoroughly, the précis of the plays they had seen. "Those poor little lovers who died together," she said. "They made it seem so right and inevitable that somehow it wasn't sad."

Martin gave her a sidelong glance. "Maybe in real life there is no sword, but ill-fated lovers are just as doomed to die . . . a living death perhaps, and isn't that more tragic?" And after a long moment's silence, he added, strangely, "There are degrees of life."

"Those nightmarish veiled figures who pulled all the strings so cleverly," Molly mused.

"They gave me the shivers," Martin admitted. "Made me realise how pertinent a symbol they were . . . each one of us on the stage of life manipulated by unseen forces. We think we act on our own volition. But do we?"

"Oh, Martin, what a dreadful idea!" Molly objected. "Are you saying we're tricked by Fate . . . have no free wills?"

He shrugged. "Sometimes it seems like that."

There was a long silence, while he gazed into space, his expression sombre, and it came to Molly as clearly as if he had spoken that he was thinking of his relationship with Solita. He didn't want to marry her—not really, in spite of the physical fascination she exercised over him. But he had been trapped into a feeling of responsibility for her, because of her illness and his own luckless part in its cause? A nervous breakdown? An attempted suicide? Impulsive as Solita might be, Molly couldn't imagine her involved in *that*—she was much too positive and aggressive a character to seek so negative a solution to her problems. However, whatever had happened to her during those months in New York after Martin left her had enabled her to forge chains with which she could now tie him to her ... for life.

"Look back," he was saying. "Haven't you ever been pushed around by circumstances wholly beyond your control?"

She gave him a long, pondering glance. "In some ways, yes ... But I like to think I have a certain amount of say-so."

He made a grimace. "Well, go on thinking it, if it comforts you."

"I don't want comfort, I want the truth," Molly asserted, with a sudden intimation that what she might say now was all-important. "There are people," she went on, "who quite obviously make life do what they want, and other folk to whom things just ... happen." She flicked him a nervous glance and wondered if she dared to go on. "Solita, for instance. Can you imagine her sitting back and letting the Fates, whoever they may be, dictate to her?"

Martin gazed at her with a sort of awe, as though he had been visited by an unexpected revelation. "You're right, Molly! Absolutely right. No Fate could manipulate Solita Gerard ... Solita manipulates Fate!"

"Well, don't let her get away with manipulating *you*," She longed to warn him. But her courage had run out.

They drank their tea in companionable silence.

"You are a comforting person, Molly bawn," Martin

said at last. "And in some ways much too wise for your years."

There it was again : the comfortable 'Nanny' role she didn't want to play. Someone who soothed rather than stimulated. But whatever she meant to him, these moments she was spending with him were precious—all she would have to live on in the months to come.

Solita greeted them with unusual sweetness when they got back to the flat. Had they had a nice time? she enquired, and listened with apparent interest, when Martin, over the inevitable aperitif, tried to convey to her something of the magic of the show they had seen. She didn't think much of the two lovers who had died together. "So Oriental and defeatist!" she said.

I was right about her attitude towards suicide, Molly reflected.

"Were they manipulating Fate, or being manipulated by it?" Martin was asking. Solita, not understanding the drift of the question, did not answer it, and changed the subject effectively by putting her hand over Martin's and telling him she had received a letter from a friend in New York by the afternoon post. "A cutting was enclosed from a social column in one of the big dailies, linking our names together . . . yours and mine. We're getting pretty deep into it, darling," she cooed. "Soon we'll have to make a definite announcement."

Murmuring that she had things to do in the kitchen, Molly left them, wondering how Martin would deal with this latest move by the Manipulator. Probably it was Solita herself who had sent that paragraph to the New York paper, she decided. It was stupid of her to use such a crude method of coercion. Martin wasn't a man who could be coerced—and she had so many other more effective weapons in her armoury. If she played it along gently, using her physical charms, Martin was hers for the taking. Probably, with his feeling of responsibility towards her, he was hers for the taking anyway, Molly ended her musings sadly. But he was putting up a fight. Solita would have to come to him on *his* terms, not *hers*. That was why he had taken her to the Odéon this afternoon, Molly decided—a second lesson for Solita in the art of not being foolishly jealous. If he married her he wouldn't be browbeaten by her. There was bleak comfort in the thought.

It was the next afternoon that he came round to the apartment, announcing as he entered the hall that he was going off to the London office for a few days. He hadn't come to stop, he said; he was on his way to the airport.

"Will you be back from London in time to go to New York with me?" Solita, who had opened the door to him, demanded.

"Sweet, I've *told* you . . . I can't make it to New York just now."

Molly, who was in the kitchen jotting down her afternoon's shopping list, couldn't help overhearing. They were talking at the tops of their voices in the corridor right outside the kitchen door.

"You're being impossible, Martin!" Solita sounded close to tears. "Why are you going out of your way to thwart me about this? It's such a little thing I'm asking you . . ."

"It's not a little thing. You must realise, my sweet, that I can't drop my *Clarion* commitments and rush off with you to the other side of the Atlantic. I've got my career and you have yours. Time and again this is going to separate us—this is something you must learn to accept."

"Why can't you find something journalistic to do in New York? Get a roving commission, so that you could freelance either in Europe or America?"

There was what must have been an exasperated pause from Martin and then he said levelly, "Now you're talking nonsense, Solita. We've been all over this before . . ." He sounded utterly weary. But still she kept on at him, putting on her little girl voice. Molly could imagine her sidling up to Martin, luring him, pleading with him:

"It could have been such fun, darling. All that gorgeous publicity for the two of us together. A New York wedding and a gallery triumph all in one . . ."

"My wedding when I have it is not going to be part of a publicity stunt," Martin returned coldly. And then Solita let him have it, storming at him, abusing him finally ending up in tears.

In an agony of embarrassment, Molly waited for the tumult to subside. There was no way of escape from the kitchen save through the hall where the two were standing. And she couldn't even close the door without drawing attention to herself. So she held her breath and waited, while Martin comforted and cajoled and gradually Solita's sobs ceased.

"I'm not quite sure," he answered when she wanted to know how long he would be in London. "But I'll phone you . . . keep in touch."

There was a silent interval while they could have been embracing, exchanging their farewell kisses. Then he was gone.

Solita, turning from the hall door, realised suddenly that Molly was in the kitchen—had been there all the time she had been talking to Martin. She came in, her face white with fury, her green eyes glittering. There was no sign of tears in them . . . had the sobs all been put on?

"What do you mean, creeping about the place, eavesdropping?" she shouted. The blaze of anger in her glance was terrifying.

But Molly's spirit rose. "I wasn't creeping about the

place," she denied hotly. "I was here in the kitchen when you and Martin began talking just outside the door. I wasn't to know it would develop into the kind of conversation it did. And when I did realise it was all rather private there was nothing I could do. Unless," she added sarcastically, "you expected me to throw myself out of the window and land four storeys down in the Rue de la Marne."

"Now you're being impertinent," Solita snapped. "There are times when I just don't know how I stand having you about the place..."

"I can always go," Molly pointed out.

"No, you can't," Solita returned, sounding more and more exasperated. "You've got both Uncle John and Martin on your side... and you know it. If it came to an open row neither of them would ever understand what it is I have against you, and I'm certainly not going to have you running to either one of them with your story of being 'turned out' by an unreasonable Solita. If you leave here, it's because you want to leave ... letting me down during my last few busy days before I take off for New York. That wouldn't sound so good, would it?"

Molly didn't answer. The whole thing was so twisted ... and *vulgar* that it made her feel faintly sick. Poor, poor Martin, she thought. Was he to spend the rest of his life in this atmosphere of half-truths and downright lies? Solita was so devious! So determined to get her own way in everything that she didn't care what crooked methods she employed.

Now she was saying, "Anyway, you probably misunderstood every single word we were saying to one another. We've discussed our careers time and again, and nothing would induce me to interfere with Martin's. It's just that I think I might be able to help him, if he came to New York. I have so many important contacts there in the newspaper world. My family, in fact, part owns one of the most important dailies in Chicago ..." She was puffing herself out as she spoke, building herself and her own importance up once more.

"But he's so independent, poor lamb," she ended. "Wanting to get by on his own efforts—and all honour to him. Being Martin one wouldn't expect anything else. However I'm not giving up. As soon as I get to New York I can pull strings, get him a tempting offer. I'm sure he'll see it my way in the end."

It won't be your fault if he doesn't, Molly thought bitterly, as she watched Solita flounce off.

A *tête-à-tête* dinner was going to be rather uncomfortable that evening. Molly hoped against hope that someone would call for the aperitif hour and be invited to stay on and eat, or else that Solita would decide to go out. But neither of these things happened and at eight o'clock she served the soup with which they usually started the evening meal. Solita consumed her portion in silence, and then said suddenly as Molly was bringing in the grilled steak, "One of the main door keys is missing."

Molly didn't take in the full significance of this remark at first.

"You have been using a single key recently ... haven't you noticed?" Solita pursued.

"Yes, I have ... vaguely," Molly answered. "I thought you'd probably had the second key taken off its ring for some reason. It was madly clumsy to carry about ..."

"*I* didn't have it taken off the ring, but *somebody* did," Solita returned darkly.

"Madame Garcia perhaps," Molly suggested. "So that she could let herself in in the mornings."

"She comes after the main gate is unlocked."

"So what?" Molly asked, puzzled.

"So," said Solita with awful significance, "someone has helped themselves to that key for their own purpose. And I don't know how long it's been missing. I happened to go to the fruit bowl on the sideboard just now to look for some papers I'd put there, and I noticed there were only two keys. You are sure you haven't got the third one in your handbag?"

"Quite sure!" Molly asserted, growing more and more mystified.

"Do you realise what it means if one of these keys is lost?" Solita asked in a voice of doom.

Molly looked at her blankly.

"It means that every house and apartment in this courtyard is exposed to the risk of burglary. The whole point of that great barricaded gate is to make illegal entry at nights impossible. Do I have to remind you," she went on, her voice rising, "that our neighbours are rich... important? A tempting prize for intruders. There are Madame Delormé's famous jewels for example, to say nothing of Monsieur le Ministre's vulnerability to any political enemy who might want to take a pot shot at him."

"Gosh!" Molly breathed, aghast.

"This missing key could lead to untold trouble..."

"Then hadn't you better tell the *concierge* about it?" Molly offered sensibly. "Or have another key cut?"

"Oh, Molly, are you being deliberately stupid?" Solita expostulated. "You have no idea the row there would be if I told the *concierge* we've lost one of the keys. As for having another one cut, you must know perfectly well that would solve nothing, still leaving the missing key in the wrong hands."

"Or just mislaid," Molly put in, refusing to be stampeded into unnecessary melodrama. "Surely it will turn up sooner or later. I don't suppose for a moment anyone has taken it for sinister motives."

"Don't you?" There was a world of significance in the brief question. "Do you know that there are thieves' markets in the back streets of Paris where a lost key can be sold to potential burglars?"

Molly's eyes widened.

"When did you last have the two keys on the one ring?" Solita persisted.

"I can't remember," Molly faltered, beginning to feel guilty in spite of herself.

"Did you have them that night you went to the Caverne to meet your revolutionary friends?"

"Yes..." Molly admitted, her heart plunging sickeningly as she realised the trend of Solita's thoughts. "But if you think..."

"I think nothing. I'm just trying to get at the truth. Have you had the two keys on the one ring since that evening?"

Molly put a hand to her head. "I can't remember."

"Well, you'd better try," Solita urged on a threatening note.

Molly stood up to remove the used plates. "I'll fetch the fruit and cheese..." she murmured. There was something so ruthless and implacable in the beautiful face confronting her across the table that she was glad to escape from it, even for a brief moment or two.

In the kitchen she stood staring into space. Try as she would she couldn't remember seeing those two wretched keys on the one ring since the night she had danced at the Caverne. André and Claude had seen her home ... and Claude had snatched the keys from her when she took them out of her handbag to open the gate, jeering at the size and weight of them. Like the keys of a gaol, he had said, and gone on melodramatically: "So this is the way the rich make themselves secure in their luxurious prisons." Unlocking the gate, he had rushed into the courtyard shouting ridiculously,

"Death to the aristocrats!" The old cry of the historic Revolution of 1792.

He had asked in which of 'these palaces' Monsieur le Ministre lived, adding that it would be fun to 'insert a nice little stink bomb in his august letterbox'.

Horrified though she was at the time, Molly had taken it all as so much schoolboy nonsense. And she still thought of it in that way, she assured herself staunchly. But with awful clarity she remembered now Solita's warning words to her before she went off to meet André that evening.

"Don't forget to take your keys this time," she had said. "And be careful not to lose them. It would never do if some hotheaded student got hold of them."

And now one of the keys had disappeared—a fact, Molly guessed, Solita would seize on with glee.

She has taken a violent dislike to me, Molly argued it out with herself; is stupidly jealous of me, and any stick will do with which to belabour me. What a stick the missing key might turn out to be!

How they were going to get through the rest of the meal she didn't know; sitting face to face over the dining table, choking down cheese and fruit in an uneasy silence . . . hating one another.

But an unexpected stroke of luck came to her aid— in the fat and breathless person of old Madame Picard, who was suddenly ringing the front door bell.

"I started out to come and see you ages ago, dear Solita," she explained as she followed Molly into the *salle-à-manger*, "thinking to have an aperitif with you, and a little chat, but believe it or not there is not one single taxi to be found on the streets of Paris tonight . . . the taxi men are staging one of their lightning strikes."

So, ignoring her bulk and her eighty-three years, she had walked the two long miles from the quiet *cul-de-*

sac off the Boulevard Montparnasse where she lived surrounded by her famous husband's paintings.

"The whole town seems to be in an uproar," she sighed, not without a certain relish, as she accepted Solita's invitation to sit down and have a belated dinner. By the time Molly brought in what was left of the soup, she was well away, vividly describing the scene on the boulevards.

"Police everywhere," she recounted, "and those horrible *wagons* of theirs tucked away in every side street with guns no doubt at the ready. Helicopters are buzzing about overhead. Sooner or later there is going to be the most awful upheaval here in Paris!"

"Wasn't it a little unwise of you to come out in the circumstances?" Solita asked reasonably enough.

"I know, my dear." Madame Picard giggled happily. "But one gets so bored sitting alone all through a long evening, and I did so want to find out how your New York plans are going. I was afraid you might be rushing off before I had seen you again. What I really want to know is what you would like for a wedding present."

Molly, happening to catch Solita's eye, looked away hurriedly. Solita's face was rigid, but her tone was all sweetness as she answered, "*Dear* Madame Picard, how lovely of you! But we haven't actually fixed a date for our wedding as yet. Martin is having some difficulty getting away from his work on the *Clarion*. They think so highly of him and are reluctant to let him go. At the moment he is over in London trying to make them see his point of view. He doesn't want to let them down, you see, or leave behind any kind of ill feeling. He is one of their most brilliant men and I suppose it's natural for them to resent it a little if he moves over to the far more profitable journalistic fields on the other side of the Atlantic."

Madame Picard nodded sympathetically. "I am sure

142

it will all work out, my dear. Love will find a way!"
She brought out the cliché with an air of dazzling orig-
inality, glancing round the table for approval.

"What would suit him best, of course," Solita was enlarging, "would be a roving commission, so that we
could wander from place to place as the spirit moved
us, he and I. There happens to be a newspaper tycoon
in my immediate family circle who is ready to help him
with this . . . hence his trip to London. It's imperative
that he should be free of his London ties . . . but he's so
loyal; it's consideration for his English employers that's
holding him back."

So that was to be her version of her situation with
Martin, Molly thought, listening to the glib words in
bitterness. The slight twist. The truth that wasn't quite
the truth. The lie that wasn't quite a lie. Solita was an
expert at the art of subtle deception. Perhaps by this
time she had even persuaded herself to believe what
she was saying. Out of wishful thinking, and her implacable determination to make life—and Martin—go
the way she wanted.

It was late when Madame Picard departed, Solita
having succeeded in phoning for a taxi for her; a private
hire service she often used herself because their cars
were unlabelled and much more luxurious than the
usual runabout taxis. The appearance of one of these
cars on the streets tonight would not seem to be strike-
breaking, so old Madame Picard would get home in
safety.

"At least it is to be hoped so!" Solita said, when she
returned from seeing the old lady into the hired car.

A series of small but ominous bangs in the distance
interrupted her words. Molly, on her way to her room,
stood with her in the corridor under the shadow of the
rubber plant to listen. The Solomon Islanders glared
down at them.

More bangs sounded.

"Smoke bombs!" Solita breathed. "Things are certainly warming up in this troubled city." She gave Molly a long significant glance, her green eyes glittering.

"That missing key . . . last known to be in your possession." It was little more than a menacing whisper. In the strong overhead light her face was tired and strained, but no weariness could soften its overt ruthlessness.

"It's not a very healthy time for keys to be missing," she said, and halted a moment to let the words sink in. Or perhaps she was waiting for the sinister drone of a hovering helicopter to die away.

"Not a healthy time at all," she repeated. "So you'd better think back, Molly my dear. Think back very carefully indeed. If you can't throw some light on the possible whereabouts of that key within the next few days, at least by the end of the week, I shall have to inform the police."

CHAPTER SEVEN

THE police! Before Molly had time to make any comment, Solita offered a curt 'goodnight', and flounced off into her bedroom, slamming the door ill-temperedly behind her.

Molly went slowly to her own room and stood staring blankly at the big still-life painting over her bed. It was quite clear that Solita believed she had given the missing key to one of André's revolutionary friends, and that she had done this deliberately—to make trouble.

Was it possible that she *had*, through carelessness, allowed the all-important key to get into the students' hands? Why hadn't she checked up on the keys that night before letting the boys go? If only she could be certain that Claude had handed them both back to her! But try as she would she could not recall in detail every moment of that fateful five minutes when André and Claude had come with her into the courtyard. It had been late, and she must have been sleepy, she supposed. Not a very satisfactory conclusion, but it was the only solution of the mystery she could arrive at.

Undressing, she got into bed to lie staring wide-eyed into the darkness, trying to remember if she had seen the two keys on the one ring since that night. But she couldn't. Recently when she had been preparing to go out in the late evenings she had found the two keys lying singly in the fruit bowl in the *salle-à-manger*. Without giving the matter much thought she had decided Solita must have split the keys up in this way to save anyone having to carry the two big clumsy keys on the one ring. It was such an obvious thing to have done that

Molly could only wonder, with the corner of her mind she had given to the problem, why this had not been done long ago. Why indeed had the two monster keys ever been put on one ring? It was bad enough to accommodate one of them in any normal-sized hand-bag. It was odd, she thought now, that she had never expected to find the three keys lying singly in the fruit bowl, or wondered why there were *not* three keys. Finding the two keys she had, she supposed, concluded that Solita had the third. Wearily her thoughts went round and round, getting her nowhere.

But to call in the police. It was unthinkable that Solita would really turn to them for aid. Aggravated by the constant rioting, they were in no mood to be gentle, even over so trivial a matter as a missing key. Not that it was all that trivial. In the circumstances prevailing it could, if it were in the wrong hands, have extremely unpleasant consequences.

They'll interrogate me, Molly thought. The word sent cold shivers down her spine. There had been sensational accounts in the Paris newspapers of student interrogation by the dreaded C.R.S., the special riot police. They had, it was hinted darkly, ways of making their victims answer questions.

Tossing in her bed, Molly tried to persuade herself that she was worrying unnecessarily. Solita only wanted to frighten her. If she really wished to put the matter of the missing key to rights all she had to do was to brave the displeasure of the *concierge* and get him to have the lock on the gateway changed. But for some reason this sensible course did not seem to appeal to her.

Because she wants to make trouble for me, Molly was once more forced to conclude. If it could be put about that she was in league with young revolutionaries she would be discredited, not only in Martin's eyes, but in Uncle John's. Solita could then throw her out in deep disgrace without showing herself in an unfavourable light.

Also, Molly mused, she can enjoy watching me suffer. The whole thing was crazy. But hadn't Martin hinted that Solita's behaviour when angry could at times be irrational? And he had told her to ring him up if ever she were scared of Solita. Well, she was scared good and proper, now, but Martin was miles away in London.

Desperately her thoughts turned to André who, a few days ago, had gone sadly and tidily out of her life. She would have to call him back again . . . briefly; tell him the whole troublesome story of the missing key. It might be that he would remember what Claude had done with the keys he was waving about that night in the courtyard. Had he handed them back intact or not? At least it would be a relief to talk it all over with André, and having decided on a plan of action, Molly pulled the bedclothes over her ears to shut out the noise of a hovering helicopter, and went to sleep.

She was awakened by Madame Garcia bringing in her breakfast tray. "What a night!" the woman said, drawing back the curtains. "Bangs and shouting in the streets until all hours, and those rattling helicopters fussing about overhead. This morning there are rumours of a transport strike. Which means no buses or Métro trains, and if that is the case I won't be able to get here to work."

Only half listening to this outpouring, Molly pulled herself up out of the warm oblivion of sleep. The memory of the missing key returned to her with cruel force. Drowsiness vanished. Sharply awake, she sat up and told Madame Garcia about the key. "Have you seen it lying about anywhere?" she asked on a wild gleam of hope.

Madame Garcia shook her head. They discussed the key's mysterious disappearance at some length. "Left in

147

the open in that fruit bowl in the *salle-à-manger* anyone could have taken it," Madame Garcia pointed out.
"The workmen, for example. Weren't they in and out of
the apartment all the time they were doing the painting
here? Then there was Maria, the cook Madame dismissed soon after you came. Did she not return one day
to ask Madame for a reference? It was one morning
when you were out. Madame refused the reference and
there was a bit of a flare-up, I can tell you! Maria
sweeping out of the place saying she would make
Madame sorry for her meanness. It would have been
easy for her to get hold of one of those keys. I remember now, I showed her into the *salle-à-manger* to wait
for Madame to come and speak to her. She could have
taken the key then, and sold it since at a good profit
in the thieves' market."

"So there really is such a place!" Molly marvelled.

"Indeed there is, my dear."

"Then if some dishonest person has bought the key
from Maria, supposing she is the culprit, why have we
not been burgled yet?"

"Because the thieves," Madame Garcia returned
knowledgeably, "wait for the *grandes vacances*. That
is the month of August when Paris is empty and all the
rich folk go away to the country or to their yachts on
the Côte d'Azur. Then come the burglars with the key
which opens all." She threw up her hands in Spanish
excitement. "And *Olé!* behold the coffers are emptied,
the money and the precious jewels disappear." She
rolled her eyes upwards, relishing the drama.

It hadn't been a very comforting conversation, leaving Molly to get through the day as best she could.
André had given her his home telephone number, so
she would have to wait until after his working hours
before trying to contact him. At six o'clock, while she
was out doing the evening shopping, she went into a

bistro in the Rue de Verneuil and used the public phone box there. A woman's voice answered her call—André's mother, no doubt. A moment later André was the other end of the line. Molly asked him if he would like to meet her about nine-fifteen at Deux Magots on the Boulevard St Germain. He said he would, his young voice jubilant. His obvious delight at her invitation made Molly feel a little guilty. But she had to talk to somebody and there was no one else to turn to.

During dinner, eaten for the most part in a strained and uneasy silence, Molly told Solita of Madame Garcia's theory that any one of the workmen recently painting the apartment windows could have taken the key out of the fruit bowl. Or Maria could have stolen it.

Solita was not impressed. "The workmen were all guaranteed to be people of integrity," she declared. "Otherwise they would not have been employed by the owners of this building. It is impossible that one of them should have taken the key. Neither did Maria take it, for she came to see me before that night when you went to the Caverne to meet your doubtful associates."

Associates—a loaded, incriminating word. And how was it that Solita was so clear about her date at the Caverne? Molly wondered.

"Oh no, my dear," she was saying, "you will have to think up a more convincing explanation of the key's disappearance if you are to convince me of your innocence in this matter. I advise you to get in touch with your boy-friends and warn them that if they try anything foolish with that key they will be in real trouble. Meanwhile you had better persuade them to hand it back to you. I will give you a few more days in which to do this before I . . . take further measures."

"But, Solita, if you only knew how wrong you are . . ." Molly began.

Solita held up a silencing hand. "It's no use, Molly.

It's all so obvious. Your very manner gives you away, and you can't deny that the key has not been seen since you took it to the Caverne. Was it the nice André who persuaded you to part with it, or one of his less reputable friends? I'm not saying it didn't all begin in a burst of youthful high spirits. You may all have thought it would be fun to wake up a bunch of old fogeys with a stink bomb or two. But some of your student friends would be capable of producing more lethal weapons, and Monsieur le Ministre, as I've pointed out, is a very vulnerable target. You see the position you've put me in? If that key doesn't turn up by the end of the week it will be clearly my duty to inform the police."

After that Molly couldn't be quick enough in clearing away the dinner dishes and getting out into the sunset streets. She didn't care if Solita guessed where she was going. By this time she herself was beginning to be convinced that Claude had indeed taken the key, and that in so far as she had carelessly not noticed it at the time she too was culpable.

She walked down the Boulevard St Germain in a troubled dream, barely noticing how quiet it was this evening—no tear gas bombs or shouting, very few police *wagons*. It might have been any May evening, with the lovers strolling under the plane trees and the pavement *cafés* doing a roaring trade.

At the Deux Magots she found a couple of chairs on the open terrace which flanked the Place. A moment later André arrived. He looked so happy coming towards her that once more she felt guilty. "*Bo' soir*, Mollee," he greeted her, and taking both her hands in his own, he lifted them gallantly to his lips. His red-gold hair was newly groomed, the scent of after-shave lotion hung on the air. It was plain that he had taken a good deal of trouble over his appearance.

"So you did not altogether forget me?" he said, seating himself on the chair at her side. Molly did not answer him, feeling more and more of a monster. Across the Place the old church dreamed behind its screen of trees, lush now with their late May growth. The sky above the Gothic spire was high and clear, fat little rose-coloured clouds, like Botticelli cherubs floating across it. Swallows swooping after the evening gnats uttered their excited cries—a sound which never failed to make Molly feel as if something wonderful were about to happen. It was like the tuning up of some celestial orchestra.

But nothing wonderful was going to happen after all. She was sitting with André, sipping fruit juice, waiting for the courage to tell him she had only come to ask him about a missing key. If only he wouldn't look at her with such tender delight!

"It was so marvellous when Maman told me a Mees Winston wanted to speak to me on the phone," he was saying softly.

"André..." she interrupted him a little unsteadily, "do you remember the night we went to the Caverne to dance, and Claude and his crowd were there?"

Some of the light went out of André's eyes. He looked a little puzzled. "*Mais oui*, of course I remember. Dancing with me you were adorable..." He tried to take her hand, but she drew away from him.

"Would you like to go back there this evening?" he asked.

"Will Claude be there?"

His look of bewilderment deepened. "I don't know. It is quite likely. It is a popular meeting place with the gang just now. Why do you ask? Do you particularly want to see Claude?" His tone was lifeless.

"It might help," Molly said. She told him about the missing key. "Do you remember that night you and Claude came back to the Rue de la Marne with me, and I gave Claude two keys on one ring to open that big stiffly locked gate. He thought they—the keys—were bizarre, great hulking things large enough to unlock a gaol gate." She shivered involuntarily as she uttered the word. "He made fun of them and ran into the courtyard shouting, 'Death to the aristocrats!'."

André grinned. "He is *méchant*, that one, but he means no harm."

Molly said, "That is the last time I definitely remember having those two keys on one ring."

André looked baffled.

Molly gazed with embarrassment into her glass of apricot juice. "I just wondered if Claude had taken one key . . . just for fun. He may have thought it might be a good idea . . . a sort of student gesture . . . to let off one of his little stink bombs in the courtyard some night under the windows of Monsieur le Ministre."

To her horror André burst out laughing. "*Quelle blague!*" he said. What a joke!

"It's not at all funny," Molly said severely, "Madame Gerard is furious over the key's disappearance and is blaming me for it. I thought perhaps you would know if Claude had taken it."

André, sobering, shook his red-gold head. "I don't think it is very likely, but if it will ease your mind we will go over to the Caverne and see if we can find him."

He put a hand under her elbow, helping her up out of her chair as if she were very old, or very precious. As they left the *terrasse* she took a last lingering look at the old peaceful church and the swooping swallows. With their flashing wings they were so beautiful. In an odd way they comforted her.

They didn't talk very much as they walked through the twilit streets, bright now with lamplight. It was clear that for André their rendezvous had turned into a bitter disappointment. He had been so full of hope when

Molly suggested it. But she had only come to ask him about a missing key.

It wasn't far to the Caverne. Claude was not there. The smoky, shadowy place was half empty. All the kids were at some protest meeting at the Sorbonne, a weary-eyed waiter told them. "Making trouble, and more trouble," he added sourly, flicking a table top with the soiled napkin he carried over his arm.

They left without ordering anything, and found themselves walking aimlessly by the river bank. "Try not to worry," André counselled kindly. "I'll ask Claude about the key when I see him. Meanwhile, why doesn't Madame Gerard have the lock on the gate changed?"

"She says it would mean too much fuss ... confessing the loss to the *concierge*. Imagine the row there would be! So she would rather wait a few days. I think she's convinced I can run that key to earth if I like. And once she gets an idea in her head there's no moving her. If she says I'm responsible, then I am, and that's the end of it. And it could be that she's right," Molly sighed. "I seem to be the last person who took out the two keys on the one ring."

Leaning over the parapet, he looked down at the re-flected lights in the river. In the distance Notre Dame, floodlit on its island, was an airy fresco of towers and spires, but Molly had no heart for its beauty tonight. Refusing Andre's offer of a cup of coffee, she said she would like to go home. She knew she was hurting him, but it couldn't be helped. She had spoiled a single even-ing for him, not a whole lifetime. In a short while he would forget he had ever met her.

Solita was out when she reached the apartment. She went to bed, her heart filled with foreboding. The more she thought about it the more convinced she was that Claude had taken the key—on a momentary impulse of mischief. He might even have lost it by now, thrown it away because of its unwieldy bulk. In which case André's intervention would do no good. She would not be able to produce the key and Solita would hand her over to the police.

It was the following afternoon that she decided to take Uncle John into her confidence, tell him the whole troublesome story. Why hadn't she thought of doing this before? Even if she had to admit to him that she had been careless over the key it would be a relief to unburden her heart to him . . . ask his advice.

As she was leaving the apartment soon after lunch Solita was in the hall, watering the rubber plant. "Where are you going?" she demanded rudely, but with an oddly nervous edge to her voice.

Quelling the impulse to answer equally rudely, "Mind your own business!" Molly said she was going to see her Uncle John.

"You aren't going to bother him with this silly story about the missing key?" Solita demanded sharply.

"Silly?" Molly echoed.

"Of course it's silly. All you have to do is to get it back from your boy-friends and the whole matter will be forgotten."

"That's fine," Molly said drily. "The only drawback being that I haven't been able to find out if my boy-friends, as you call them, have the key."

"Of course they have it," Solita persisted. "It's just that you're too obstinate to admit that you gave it to them."

There was no point in answering this accusation. Brushing past Solita in the narrow hall, Molly put her hand on the latch of the hall door. Solita with a swift movement forward caught at her arm.

"Listen to me!" she said, her voice rising hysterically. "If you make trouble between me and your uncle over this you'll be sorry! You've tried to come between me

154

and Martin...now you want to turn Uncle John against me!"

This was such a distortion of the facts that Molly could only stare in amazement.

"I wish you'd never come here!" Solita stormed.

"So do I!" Molly returned with feeling. "I'll clear out if you like...right away, go back to England to-night. Nothing would please me better."

"No doubt," Solita sneered. "But you aren't going to slink off until you have returned that key. I would have you stopped at the airport."

Molly, shaking off the arresting hand, opened the door and hurried into the lift, her heart beating un-evenly. Why was Solita unwilling for Uncle John to be told about the missing key? This affair seemed to grow more inexplicable at every turn.

It was sultry and hot as she walked down the now familiar Boulevard St Germain, its great width shrieking with cars that rushed in both directions. Groups of young men in various states of unconventional attire stood about on the tree-lined pavement. There was an air of breathlessness in the thundery afternoon—as if everyone were waiting for something to happen.

Uncle John's gallery, on the contrary, was peaceful and cool. A few people drifted in and out, looking at the paintings which lined the walls—arty types mostly, but here and there elegantly dressed women lingered. Wealthy Americans, perhaps. Serious art collectors. Uncle John's middle-aged secretary, Madame Duprés, sat at her little desk in a far corner of the gallery.

"May I go through to the office and see my uncle?" Molly asked her. She nodded and smiled.

"You will find him having a little nap, I imagine. He came in very tired after lunch."

"Perhaps I ought not to disturb him, then," Molly offered.

"Oh, it is all right," Madame Duprés assured her. "It is time he was woken up; he will want to sign his afternoon letters."

Molly crossed the polished parquet floor, skirted an enormous, improbable 'mobile', and knocked lightly on Uncle John's office door. There was no response. She opened the door softly and went in. Uncle John was slumped in his chair, his head on one side in an odd strangled position, his face very red, his breathing most peculiar.

"Uncle John!" Molly cried in alarm. She touched his shoulder tentatively. He did not stir. Veins stood out on his forehead and his mouth hung open.

Thoroughly alarmed, Molly returned to the gallery and summoned Madame Duprés. "There's something wrong with my uncle ... please come!"

Madame Duprés jumped to her feet with an air of concern. "I told him he would make himself ill," she said as they hurried across the shining floor. "He was rushing about in the heat all this morning getting Solita's huge canvases off to the States. There was some trouble at the Customs ..."

Together they entered the little office. The old gentleman was still in the same unnatural position and all their efforts failed to rouse him. Madame Duprés loosened his tie and found a cushion for his head, then told Molly to telephone for the doctor.

Fortunately he lived near, and came quickly. Uncle John, he pronounced, had had a slight seizure. There was no cause for undue alarm. A week or two of rest in a nursing home should put him to rights.

Waiting for the ambulance to arrive, Molly felt as if the bottom had dropped out of her world. Not until this moment had she realised how much it meant to her having Uncle John behind her in Paris, perhaps most especially as a buffer between herself and the incalculable Solita . . . now at her most venomous. But Uncle John could no longer be relied on to come to the rescue.

She went with him in the ambulance and to her immense relief he partly regained consciousness. The doctor, who had accompanied them, was triumphant. "What did I tell you, *mademoiselle*? Your uncle is already making the recovery. A good rest and he will be none the worse. At his age," he added with a head-shake, "he should not eat or drink too generously at midday, especially when a heavy afternoon's work lies ahead of him."

By the time Molly left the old gentleman comfortably settled in the nursing home he was fully conscious but very exhausted.

"He must not be worried by any business or family concerns for at least a fortnight," the doctor had warned.

Under the influence of the tranquillising drugs he had been given he seemed to accept the situation calmly. "A silly business," he murmured drowsily as Molly kissed him goodbye. "I can't think what possessed me to faint like that. But it will be nice to rest for a few days. Tell Solita she's not to worry, that I'll soon be all right. She may come and see me, if she likes . . ."

But Solita did worry, selfishly, when Molly returned to the apartment and told her what had happened. "What foul luck!" she exclaimed. "Just at this moment, when I was depending upon him to see to the business side of this transfer of my paintings to New York!"

"It was fussing over your canvases," Molly burst out indignantly, "that brought on his illness. He spent all morning in the heat arguing with the Customs . . . dashing back and forth across Paris. . . . But you don't care!"

For once Solita seemed robbed of the power of speech. Molly's attack had floored her—perhaps because of the undeniable degree of truth in it.

"He said you could go and see him if you wished,"

Molly went on. "Not that you will," she added with wild disregard for the consequences. "Unless it suits you. You never think of anyone but yourself."

Like all bullies when attacked Solita was completely taken aback. But the look she darted at Molly as she walked away was charged with pure hatred. If looks could have killed! Molly, beginning to regret her impetuous outburst, felt cold terror clutch at her heart. With Uncle John laid low and Martin in London Solita could have her moment of revenge uninterrupted. And that missing key would be a godsend!

CHAPTER EIGHT

THE atmosphere was pretty grim at 64b Rue de la Marne the following day. Solita, refusing to eat with Molly, had her lunch sent into the studio on a tray. Fortunately she was out for dinner. Molly ate hurriedly and then went off to the Caverne in search of Claude. This time she found him there with his companions, sitting round a table scattered with the inevitable litter of glasses and cigarette ash. He greeted her with a warmth which surely indicated a clear conscience.

"The Commune is in session! Come and join us. Comrade Léon is giving us a talk on guerilla tactics in street fighting."

This was obviously supposed to be funny. Everybody laughed. But Comrade Léon, an older man than the rest, bearded and swarthy, looked sinister enough to be an authority on any kind of violence. Molly took an instinctive dislike to him.

"I haven't come to stay," she said, perching in a transitory fashion on the edge of a chair one of the boys had pulled up for her. Then she told Claude about the missing key. His young face remained innocently blank.

"There were two keys on one ring," Molly reminded him. "Did you give them both back to me that night I handed them to you to open the gate at my home?"

He frowned as though trying to recall the incident. "Those great iron keys with which you lock yourself into your *bourgeois* retreat? Yes, I'm sure the two keys were still on the one ring when I gave them back to you."

"You didn't detach one and keep it, for a joke?" Molly pursued.

"*Mais non!*" Claude sounded hurt. "What do you take me for, a thief? And anyway, what would I want with one of your keys?"

Molly didn't remind him of his little pleasantry about throwing stink bombs through the letter box of Monsieur le Ministre, and very soon after that she left the group and made her way back to the empty apartment.

So Claude could be ruled out as the villain of the piece. Or could he? As she lay awake that night worrying, her doubts of Claude returned. She had no evidence that he hadn't been simply fobbing her off this evening at the Caverne—warned beforehand perhaps by André that she was on the warpath, looking for the key. That character with the black beard looked every inch an anarchist, and would be only too glad to add to his repertoire of horrors by staging a little terrorism in the courtyard of the apartments on the Rue de la Marne.

The next morning she walked aimlessly in the Tuileries Gardens. The glorious weather still held and the cooing of the pigeons was a cool and soothing sound in the midday heat. Children raced with their hoops. In the little theatre under the trees the Guignol puppets worked out their tiny destinies, and away over the Louvre white clouds floated in a summer sky. It was all as lovely as ever, but Molly had no heart for it. The week of grace Solita had granted her was drawing to a close and the mystery of the missing key remained unsolved. Would she really send for the police? And if she did, what then? Molly could see herself being bundled into one of the terrifying squat-nosed *wagons* and whipped away to some ghastly commissariat to be questioned. Vague visions of torture floated through her mind. "When did you last have the key? What are the names of your accomplices?"

It was so improbable a situation for her to imagine herself in that she could almost have laughed, only that it was no laughing matter.

Once more she ate a solitary lunch while Solita sulked in the studio—a ridiculous state of affairs. It couldn't go on. Molly went to her room and flung herself on her bed, the interminable hours of the afternoon stretching ahead of her. If she hadn't been afraid of annoying Solita and Madame Garcia she would have fetched brooms and vacuum cleaner and scrubbing brush and cleaned out her neglected, dusty room. But she had put up with it in its present state so long, she could endure it for the short while that remained to her. If only she knew what date had been fixed for Solita's departure to New York! No doubt she was waiting for Martin to finalise his plans, sever his conection with the *Clarion* in London. If that was really what he was doing.

But there's no need for *me* to wait, Molly thought suddenly. She could get up off this bed and walk out of the apartment at this very moment . . . slip away secretly back to England. The thought brought her to her feet, her heart beating quickly. All she had to do was pack her bags and walk out. She wasn't Solita's prisoner. "I'll have you stopped at the airport if you try to run away," she had threatened. But if she managed it cleverly Solita wouldn't miss her until she was well on her way. Anyway, she wouldn't go by air; she couldn't afford to. Counting the francs in her handbag, she saw that she had just about enough to buy her a train and boat ticket. Once she reached home she had savings in the Post Office that would see her through until she found another job. She might even phone Martin at the *Clarion* and ask him to speak to Mr Prendergast for her . . . she would tell him the whole stupid story of the missing key and Solita's threats—a prospect which brought colour to her cheeks and sent her spirits soaring.

Then she remembered Uncle John, and felt a little guilty. During her walk this morning she had phoned the nursing home to be told that Monsieur Pembury was resting comfortably and that the doctor was satisfied with his progress. When she suggested coming to see him, the nurse to whom she was speaking said that the doctor advised complete rest, and no visitors for at least a week. "Well, give him my love, and tell him I'll come as soon as the doctor lets me."

Now, if she ran away, she would have to write to him instead and explain what had happened. He knew Solita's unpredicability and might not be surprised. Molly felt sure he would understand her predicament, and even if he thought she was panicking needlessly, he would forgive her. It wasn't as if he expected a great deal in the way of attention from her; he was an independent old boy. She and her mother had never been very close to him. His life was far out of their humble orbit and he had never shown any signs of needing them. He was comfortably off and self-sufficient, and moreover, if he really wanted her fussing round him in his illness, he would, Molly told herself, be quite capable of sending for her and paying her fare back to Paris. But it was hardly likely that he would do this.

The pealing of the hall door bell interrupted her thoughts. Hurrying to answer the summons, she found a dapper, middle-aged Frenchman, very correct in black jacket and pin-striped trousers—the invariable uniform of the Parisian business man. He carried a briefcase under his arm. Removing his soft wide-brimmed black hat, he bowed courteously. "I have an appointment with Madame Gerard," he announced.

"Won't you come in?" Molly invited. "I'll see if she is at home."

"Is that Monsieur Musset?" came Solita's voice brightly, as she emerged from her bedroom, looking fresh and radiant as if she had just wakened from a peaceful afternoon nap. "*Entrez, monsieur* ... so good of you to come so promptly," she said, leading her visitor into the salon, and closing the door firmly behind her. Whatever these two had to say to one another was evidently confidential.

Would the visitor be invited to stay for tea? Molly wondered. It was just about time for Solita's afternoon tray. But Molly did not like to interrupt the discussion going on in the salon. She could hear vaguely Monsieur Musset's resonant French voice droning on and on ...

Going into the kitchen she made out her evening shopping list. Was Solita going to be in to dinner or not? If only she would say! This punishment by sulky silence was intolerable. Molly knew she couldn't take much more of it.

Soon she heard Monsieur Musset being shown out. His stay had been too brief for a social call. "I have an appointment," he had said when he arrived, as if he had come on business of some kind. A travel agent with the New York tickets, perhaps. Not particularly interested, Molly went off to do her shopping as soon as she had taken Solita her five o'clock coffee.

As usual, her walk through the lively Rue de Verneuil refreshed her. She enjoyed her passing contacts with the quick-moving, forceful French housewives—women, she thought wistfully, who would go home with their appetising purchases to eat companionably with their families. Dreading her own lonely evening, she returned to the apartment. Never had it seemed more uninviting. Her resolution to run out on it all began to strengthen. The strange paintings shouldering one another off the grimy walls; it must be years since the place had been redecorated; the shadowy ill-kept rooms ... what a relief it would be to get away from it all! Yet by any standards it was a luxurious home—bought for Solita by her wealthy father. It was simply that with an artist's bohemian disregard for all things domestic she didn't care how the place was kept. Poor Martin! Whatever gifts Solita might bring to their union, housekeeping wasn't going to be one of them.

When Molly wheeled the dinner trolley into the salon she was lying on the settee with the telephone receiver in her hand—talking to him. At least so Molly concluded. Only Martin could bring that smug look of satisfaction to her lovely face. She had him well and truly where she wanted him—even at the end of a line stretched across a few hundred miles of land and water.

"Darling," she was saying now to whatever he was telling her, "I can't believe it. Oh, darling, how marvellous!" Her green eyes softened, and something like tenderness lit her beautiful face. She *is* in love with him, Molly thought sadly. That's what's making her hate me so much. She can't bear it when Martin is nice to me. The fact that I once typed memoranda for him in a London office is intolerable.

Leaving the dishes covered on the trolley, she went out of the room to eat her own solitary meal in the *salle-à-manger*.

Later when she was piling the used crockery on the draining-board beside the sink for Madame Garcia to see to in the morning, Solita came into the kitchen. She had changed into a frock of oriental design, a black background with great splashes of vivid colour. Barbaric ear-rings swung from her ears. "I'm going to a party at Madame Picard's," she announced, condescending for once to disclose her destination. "She asked me to bring you along too, but I declined for you. I thought it better so. It's too awkward for us to go out together in the present circumstances."

164

Molly turned from the sink, colouring up with resentment. "I . . . like Madame Picard," she began inadequately. How dared Solita refuse invitations for her without consulting her?

"Things can't go on as they are," she was saying. And after an ominous pause: "That was my lawyer who called this afternoon. I've told him the very odd story of the missing key and he advises me to put the matter in the hands of the police without delay." She watched with a sort of cruel glee as Molly turned pale. Then she went on with a magnanimous air, "But I'll give you twenty-four hours more in which to produce that key—or at least tell me where it is. Handing you over to the police just now would, I realise, be a serious step. They have so much trouble to cope with in the streets that they're not in the best of tempers. So there it is . . . you tell me where that key is by this time tomorrow or . . . take the consequences."

Without giving Molly time to reply to this ultimatum she walked out of the kitchen. Molly stared after her in a hypnotised fashion. The police! So it had come at last. With shaking hands she finished stacking the dishes, then went to her room and sat down on her bed, covering her face with her hands. Beyond her open windows the evening sky was rosy. The eternal swallows swooping and calling through the gentle air seemed like the music of some other world. The voice of the real world was the whirr of a police helicopter hovering over the seething boulevards.

Fighting back the paralysing waves of fear, Molly forced herself to face the issue calmly. There were no doubts in her mind now as to what she ought to do. While Solita was out of the way this evening she would slip away, find a night train that would get her to the coast . . . She had only the vaguest idea when the Channel steamers sailed, but she could easily phone the

Gare St Lazare and find out. Even if she got no further than Boulogne tonight she would surely be safe.

But when she got through to the enquiry office at the station, she was told curtly that there were no trains to the coast tonight. The man's manner was so offhand that she did not pursue the matter, concluding that the last boat train had gone. She did not resent, or find it extraordinary, the way the railway official had spoken to her. In France officials are so often curt and even downright rude. In any case she was too busy assessing the situation to bother about a few hard words. She couldn't get away now until first thing in the morning. She would leave the apartment even before Madame Garcia arrived. Solita was seldom out of her room before noon . . . By which time, with any luck, she would be well on her way.

She spent the rest of the evening packing her things. Putting them into her two suitcases gave her already a sense of release. Later she got into bed and lay waiting for the dawn to break—she was too excited to sleep, save in light snatches. At one point she heard Solita come in and go to her room. The long hours dragged on. Never had a sunrise been more welcome!

It was just before eight o'clock when she stole out of the apartment, lugging her two heavy cases. Fortunately the *concierge* was not in his lodge, and the wicket gate was already unlocked, so she was able to creep out into the street unobserved. All she had to do now was to cross the road to a nearby taxi rank and take a cab to the Gare St Lazare. She could hardly believe that in less than twelve hours she would be safely back in Chiswick . . . this Paris nightmare behind her.

The cab rank, she saw then, was empty. Putting down her cases, she waited for one of the cabs to return. It was rather odd for them all to be engaged so early in the day. Moments ticked by, until almost half an hour had elapsed. Gradually Molly became aware of the little knots of people gathering round the newsagent's shop across the way, talking excitedly. On the posters displayed was the one enormous word *'Grève'!* That meant 'Strike'. Perhaps the taxi men were now once more joining in the general upset by staging another of their strikes. Picking up her cases, she made her way to the corner *bar-tabac* which had so often during the past few weeks been her refuge. The woman behind the counter greeted her familiarly.

"You were intending to travel today, *mademoiselle*?" she queried, eyeing the suitcases. "*Tiens!* But you have the bad luck. A General Strike has been declared. Hadn't you heard? All transport ceased at midnight, even the planes at Orly are grounded, the Grandes Lignes are immobile, the stations shut, as well as the Métros."

Molly sank down on one of the chairs by a fablon-topped table, her legs giving way beneath her.

"Paris is closed to the world," the woman behind the counter announced with a certain macabre relish. "Paris is for the moment *un grand prison* from which there is no escape. It is to be hoped this fact does not derange you too seriously, *mademoiselle*."

CHAPTER NINE

MOLLY'S first reaction was one of stunned disbelief. This couldn't be happening to her . . . it was too much to take in. She looked round the *tabac* with a hunted air, feeling herself trapped. Nothing would induce her to go back to the apartment; but where else *could* she go? "How long will the strike last?" she asked foolishly— for how could the *tabac* woman possibly know?

Her answer was inevitably a shrug. "Who can say? It could be the beginning of serious trouble, or, as one says, 'the flash in the pan'. Would you care for a cup of coffee? You look as if you could do with one. This has given you a shock . . ."

"It is very important that I should leave for England today," Molly explained. "And yes, please, I should like some coffee." In her hurry to get away she had not stopped to make any breakfast and pangs of hunger were beginning to make themselves felt.

When the woman brought the coffee, with a plate of brioches, she laid a newspaper on the table. "This has just come. It will give you the latest news of the situation."

After a few mouthfuls of the hot reviving coffee Molly studied the headlines, and found them disturbing. A leading article depressingly explored the predictable results of the stoppage. But the writer did not feel it would last long. Labour unrest and student protest did not march side by side. The trades unions were not in favour of such a coalition.

If only Martin were here with his informed journalist's access to all that was going on! But the thought of him brought inspiration. There was nothing to stop her going to the *Clarion* office, which was within walking distance, and making herself and her plight known to some sympathetic member of the staff. She could say she was a friend of Martin Varney's, and that she had once worked at the London office. With suddenly soaring hopes it occurred to her that they would surely know what steps were being taken to get stranded tourists out of Paris. At this time of the year hundreds of overseas visitors were on the move. It might even be that they would be making private arrangements for the movements of their own staff. It was part of a newspaperman's job to keep rushing from one place to another.

"Do you mind if I leave my luggage here for half an hour or so?" she asked the café proprietress. "I've thought of somebody who might be able to tell me if there are any emergency services going into operation. There must be many travellers in Paris today as stranded as I am."

"Go to one of the main line stations," the woman advised. "I'm told there may be coaches going from the central station yards to Ostend or Brussels, where you could pick up a cross-Channel boat. You are very welcome to leave your cases here." She carried them to safety in a room behind the counter.

It was strangely quiet walking along the short side street which led to the river. There were no buses, no commuters hurrying to work. And it was apparently too early for any political or police activity. Protesters and demonstrators would get up late, Molly supposed, having spent most of the hours of darkness roaming the streets, or talking themselves hoarse in all-night cafés. A few police *wagons* were lined up on the bridges, and the usual barges fussed up and down the Seine. The fishermen, she noticed, were already to be seen on the lower of the two towpaths. She wondered if they ever went home. They never looked up from their fishing lines, never spoke to one another. Strikes and riots and baton charges flowed over their unconcerned heads. Patiently they waited for the fish which never came.

Taking the Pont de la Concorde, she came to the Rue Royale. It was odd to see all the big shops shuttered and closed. The travel agency near the Madeleine was firmly shut, so it was no use hoping for information from that quarter. But her hopes were fixed on the people at the *Clarion*; they were the lifeline to which she now clung! The line of cars and vans drawn up outside the main entrance was reassuring—distribution of the morning's issue would, it seemed, go on. With a heart that had gone suddenly much lighter she entered the swinging glass doors.

But the clerk at the reception desk wasn't very helpful. Hardly anyone was about yet, he told her, and she remembered that newspaper editorial staff, like the student protesters, worked late and wouldn't be likely to arrive at the office before early afternoon.

"I am a friend of Mr Varney's," she offered persuasively. "If there is just *someone* I could speak to for a moment. I'm stranded here by the strike ... trying to get home to England ..."

"There is a young lady who at times does secretarial work for Mr Varney, a Mademoiselle Lavelle," the clerk suggested. (A French Molly Winston, Molly thought.) "I'll see if she is available."

A few moments later Molly found herself confronting a pleasant-looking girl about her own age. "I am held up by the strike," she repeated, "and as I am a friend of Mr Varney's and was one time a member of the *Clarion* staff in London, I wondered if anybody here could help me to get away."

The girl, sitting behind her typewriter, looked doubtful. "The emergency has hit us so suddenly," she said. "I'm afraid nothing has yet been arranged to meet it. I expect we shall get round to organising some kind of transport for our own people by tomorrow . . ."

"But I want to get away at once," Molly put in desperately, ignoring that fact that she could hardly be classed as one of their 'own people'.

"You haven't a car, I suppose?" the girl said. "I'm told it's possible to find boats still in action if you can get to the coast."

Molly shook her head. She hadn't a car, she confirmed sadly.

Mademoiselle Lavelle pondered the situation for a moment, then said kindly, "I'm sure the Editor would like us to help you if we can. I'll have a word with him when he comes in' . . . which will be soon, I expect, seeing the way things are. Would you care to leave me your telephone number?"

Molly's thoughts whirled. Where could she go while she waited for the call? Could she possibly creep back into the flat before Solita had had time to get up? It was still too early for her to be about. Last night she had spoken of contacting the police 'in twenty-four hours'. That meant there was still almost a whole day to play with. And with the fresh turn in events the police might be too busy to bother with what could only sound like a case of petty theft. Finding herself here at the *Clarion* among people who would be ready to help her if they could had given her fresh courage. Perhaps she had been foolish to try to 'run away'—an undignified proceeding. It would be better to face up to Solita, tell her she was returning to England—with the help of the powerful *Clarion*—and let her do her damnedest. This police threat had been going on for so long. Maybe it was no more than a threat. When you thought about it calmly there was something very peculiar about the way Solita had been behaving over this business of calling the police. Something vaguely unreal. If she was going to do it at all why hadn't she done it long ago?

"Could we phone you where you are staying?" Miss Lavelle prompted.

It would be awkward if Solita took the call. "I'd better phone you, I think," Molly suggested. "I'm not very certain of my movements this morning. But I could call you . . . say about one o'clock?" She could do that from the convenient *bar-tabac*, she thought.

Miss Lavelle smiled. "*Bien!* I am sure we shall have some kind of transport laid on sooner or later, and as you are an ex-member of the staff I'm certain Mr Grantley, the Editor, will do what he can for you."

Molly's spirits once more soared. She felt as if she were already half way home. "How is Mr Varney?" she couldn't stop herself asking. It sounded rather foolish, so she added hurriedly, "I hope he is enjoying his London assignment."

"Oh, he is," Miss Lavelle said. "He has been through on the phone several times and seems to be in great form. As a matter of fact I was talking to him yesterday and he told me he will be staying on in London for a while yet as he has been asked to cover an important conference on modern architecture."

Which would give her time to see him when she got to London, Molly thought. Walking back to the Rue de la Marne she felt more cheerful than she had for days. It looked as if her troubles were almost over. It would be marvellous to see the last of Solita and her gloomy apartment. She was sure she could get back into it now, unseen. There wouldn't even be a Madame Garcia to ask awkward questions, since she would have been unable to get her usual bus to work. Luckily Molly still had the hall door key in her handbag, having forgotten to leave it behind when she stole out of the place this morning. She would have had to return it by post, she supposed. By this time, she thought with a nervous giggle, Solita will have got used to my habit of stealing keys!

Confident that things would work out, she collected her bags from the *bar-tabac*, told the woman there that she had almost arranged a lift by car to the coast, and walked the few steps to 64b. When she reached the hall door she inserted her key cautiously and turned the lock. An instant later she found herself face to face with Solita, who was coming out of the kitchen with her breakfast tray. The green eyes were emerald-hard.

"So you decided to come back," she said, with a sneering glance at the suitcases. "How very foolish of you to try to run away . . . sealing beyond any doubt your guilt."

Molly, taken by surprise, could only stare at her, speechless. "There were no trains," she brought out at last.

"I know." Solita laughed nastily. "I had a job to get a taxi to bring me back from the party last night. The driver told me the strike had already started. I went to your room just now to tell you we should have no Madame Garcia to see to breakfast, and I saw that all your things had been removed. I guessed you were trying to do a flit, but knew you wouldn't get very far." She put her tray down on the table beside the rubber plant. "Give me that key you have in your hand," she ordered. Molly handed it over and going to the hall door Solita locked it and put the key in her negligée pocket. "You will not run away again so easily," she said. "Meanwhile I'd be glad if you would make some fresh toast. I've burned this lot . . ." With a characteristic toss of her head she walked off to her room, tray in hand.

Molly picked up her suitcases and carried them into her room. She could have wept with sheer frustration. Fancy Solita being about so early. And that melodramatic gesture, locking the hall door. But I'll get away somehow, Molly resolved fiercely. There were the *Clarion* people, ready to help her with a car. For she had quite made up her mind by this time that this was as good as settled. If it came to the worst *she* would do a bit of police calling, report that she was being 'unlawfully detained'. The phrase had a reassuringly legal ring. As for the business of the missing key, she was ready to answer any questions the police might put to her. There wasn't, she assured herself, in her fresh mood of courage, any real evidence that she was responsible for the key's disappearance. The whole thing had been built up by Solita to intimidate her. The pity was that she had allowed herself to be intimated to the extent of trying to run away, a mistake she now regretted.

When she took the toast in to Solita she was reclining gracefully in bed, reading a detective novel. The telephone, which could be carried from room to room, was plugged in on her bedside table. Molly looked at it hungrily, wondering how she could get hold of it to phone Miss Lavelle at one o'clock, as she had promised. She would just take it, she resolved, and ring up the *Clarion*, the police . . . anyone she felt like ringing.

"Listen, Solita," she began firmly. "It was silly of me to creep off this morning, like the criminal I am not. But you'd better know I have no intention of remaining locked up in this apartment. I'm leaving for London this afternoon. My friends at the *Clarion* office are arranging it for me. I'm to phone them at one o'clock . . ."

Solita, maddeningly, went on reading her book. Without looking up she said, "I'm not sure that you'll be here at one o'clock. I've just spoken to the police and they're sending someone round to interrogate you as soon as possible. So I shouldn't try to do anything foolish, if I were you."

Ashamed of the sudden wild beating of her heart, Molly fought for control, clenching her hands. "I shall be very glad to speak to the police," she declared defiantly. "It may be that they'll have something to say to you about locking me up. I'm sure it's an illegal thing to do . . . probably looked on as a form of personal assault."

Solita just went on reading, and after waiting for a moment or two in suppressed fury Molly went back to the kitchen and made herself a cup of tea.

Just how she got through the hours that followed she would never know. Ten o'clock, eleven o'clock . . . time limped on and no police appeared. Solita remained closeted in her room, listening to the news bulletins on her transistor radio. At noon Molly managed to concoct some sort of a meal from tins stored in the kitchen cupboard. Solita, up and dressed by this time, had her tray as usual in solitary state in the studio.

"No police yet," Molly couldn't help pointing out on a note of triumph, as she put the tray down on the little table that was as usual littered with brushes and tubes.

"They'll be here!" Solita asserted confidently. "I told them there was no hurry. They're naturally busy today."

Back in the kitchen Molly tried to choke down some tinned tongue and a slice of rather stale bread and butter. One o'clock came and went and she hadn't had a chance of phoning Miss Lavelle. Solita had taken the phone into the studio with her and when Molly had asked if she might use it she had refused point blank. Short of embarking on a physical struggle with her there was nothing to be done.

Molly washed up the lunch dishes, swept the kitchen floor, cleaned the sink . . . anything to keep busy. By three o'clock her nerves were at breaking point, waiting for the ring at the hall door which never came. Bravely as she had reasoned with herself, she still dreaded the arrival of the police, because they were French, incalculable and unknown, riot squads. But she wouldn't think of the things she had heard about their brutality. Just what had Solita said to them? If indeed she had spoken to them at all. Was this waiting game part of the mental torture she seemed to love to inflict? The whole situation was becoming more and more crazy.

Then, just about half past four, when she was preparing Solita's afternoon coffee tray there was a peal at the hall door bell which nearly made her jump out of her skin. It was Solita—who still had the key of the door—who hurried to answer it.

"Par ici, m'sieur!" Molly heard her say, as she led whoever it was into the salon. Then she called, "Molly, come here, please," and Molly knew it was the police. No myth after all, but a grim reality.

Holding her head high, determined not to show the fear she couldn't help feeling, she went into the salon. The man who stood awaiting her wasn't one of the dreaded riot squad, but an ordinary *agent de police*. Squat and fat, the belt about his bulging middle adorned with a baton, he looked hot and uncomfortable. Removing his cap, he wiped his red face with a grubby handkerchief.

"This is the girl I wish to charge," Solita said, as Molly entered the room.

"Bien!" growled the *agent*, putting his cap back on again. He glared at Molly with two black boot-button eyes, sizing her up in silence for a moment.

"Your name, *mademoiselle*," he demanded then, taking the inevitable notebook from his breast pocket.

"Molly Winston," Molly answered all but inaudibly.

"Spell it," the *agent* shouted. "And speak up! Now,

once more—your name? You are a foreigner? English?"
The questions rattled on.

"You are here in a domestic capacity, I understand? Have you papers of residence? A work permit? Have you at any time since entering the country reported your sojourn to the police?"

"No, no, officer," Solita interrupted with an uneasy laugh. "All this is not necessary. Miss Winston is here on a completely informal footing, merely on a brief visit."

"But in your telephoned statement you told us she worked for you . . ."

"By mutual arrangement," Solita said.

The *agent* shook his head. *"C'est pas normal!"* he muttered to himself. "All very irregular." Then turning to Molly once more: "When did you arrive in Paris, *mademoiselle*?"

"On the fifth of May," Molly told him.

He pushed back his cap and scratched his cropped skull. "You have been here more than a month working for this lady and you have filled in no papers with the police . . ."

"But surely this is beside the point," Solita broke in again. It was clear the interview was not going the way she had planned. "Miss Winston is my guest . . . my friend . . ."

Molly could hardly believe her ears.

The *agent* made an exasperated gesture. "She is your friend and you ring us up and tell us she has stolen your key!" His tone was heavily sardonic.

"A key she could have passed to a group of anarchists," Solita said desperately.

The boot-button eyes threw her a look of scorn. "So! Your English friend is an anarchist . . ."

"I didn't say that!"

"Then, in heaven's name, what did you say?" thundered the *agent*.

A sound from the hall reached their ears. Someone was entering by the door Solita had apparently, in her excitement when she had admitted the policeman, left on the latch.

"Anybody at home?" a familiar voice called out, and an instant later Martin Varney was walking into the salon.

CHAPTER TEN

"MARTIN!" Solita cried. Her voice held more of alarm than of welcome. She stretched her hands out to him, but ignoring the gesture, he asked abruptly, "What does this policeman want here? What are you doing to Molly?"

"Who is this man?" the *agent* wanted to know simultaneously.

"My fiancé," Solita returned—a word with more than one meaning in French parlance. The policeman grunted.

"Just what on earth is going on?" Martin demanded in bewilderment, his brow darkening as his gaze came to rest on Molly's pale and frightened face. She hadn't yet fully taken in the miracle of his appearance. Things were happening too quickly.

"What indeed is going on? You may well ask, *m'sieur*!" The *agent* turned to the newcomer with an air of relief—a man of the world from whom he might hope to get some sense. "Here I am with a General Strike on my hands, the students storing their petrol bombs and paving stones on the rooftops for the night's barrage, and this good lady here..." he indicated Solita with a sneer, "sends for me because she has had a quarrel with her girl friend, whom she accuses of stealing a key! A key! I ask you. And Paris on the brink of red revolution!"

"But that is the whole point," Solita broke in eagerly. "Molly...Miss Winston...has foolishly let one of the keys of our outer gate get into the hands of her revolutionary student friends. One of them, she calmly told me, makes bombs. What is to prevent him—with the aid of our missing key—from blowing up the house of the Government Minister who lives across the courtyard?"

"They are only stink bombs," Molly put in.

The policeman began to write in his notebook again.

"*Did* you give a key to one of your student friends?" Martin asked Molly, but his voice was gentle.

"I'm ... not sure," Molly answered, realising how stupid and evasive it must sound. "It all happened about a fortnight ago. I went to a discothèque called La Caverne with André Colbert and met some of his friends. One of them, named Claude, the one who makes the stink bombs, came with us when André saw me home. I gave him the two keys on one ring to unlock the outer gate—as it's difficult to manage and sometimes sticks. I can't remember if he gave me both the keys back. I didn't notice at the time ... it was very late and I was tired. And I'm afraid I didn't think about it since, until Solita discovered the third key was not in the fruit bowl in the *salle-à-manger* where the keys are kept."

"What is the full name of this Claude?" the *agent* asked.

"It is all right, officer," Martin interrupted. "I think I can clear up this little mystery. I believe I know where the missing key might be. Madame Gerard will not be needing your services any more. We are sorry to have troubled you."

The *agent* glared at Solita. "You withdraw the charge against this Mees Winston?"

"But of course, if my fiancé has the missing key. I must confess that was a solution which did not occur to me." She gave the *agent* her most winning smile. "I'm most terribly sorry for having bothered you."

"I should think so!" grumbled the policeman, and stalked out of the salon, down the corridor and out of the hall door, which he slammed behind him resentfully.

There was an interval of strained silence, during which Molly was conscious only of the waves of relief washing over her. So Martin had the missing key! What a simple and natural solution to the mystery . . . and he had dropped out of the skies like an angel of deliverance to make it known to them, just in the nick of time. A few minutes later and she might have been bundled off by the indignant little *agent*, who had obviously been impressed by the revolutionary bit in Solita's story.

"Darling, how wonderful of you to walk in just when I needed you so badly," Solita was saying. Going over to him, she put her two hands appealing on his arm. But he was still oddly unresponsive. "How did you manage to get away from those tiresome editors in London?" she asked. "I thought you had to remain in England for some days yet, to attend some stupid architectural conference."

"I was supposed to," Martin's voice was coldly controlled. "But I happened to phone the office here early this morning and spoke to Miss Lavelle, my part-time secretary. She told me Molly had just been to the *Clarion*, asking if they could help her to get out of Paris as it was urgent that she should leave at once. I guessed she must be in some kind of serious trouble . . . and I flew over right away to see what I could do to help."

Solita drew back sharply, her face going crimson with outrage, her whole air changing. "You came rushing back here to help *Molly Winston*!" The incredulity and scorn in her tone made Molly wince.

"That's right," Martin was confirming quietly. "I came because, as I said, I sensed she was in big trouble of some kind and I guessed it was you who was making it for her. It hasn't escaped me how maliciously you've often felt about her."

He took an almost menacing step towards Solita, his

face darkening. "You would have handed her over to the police!" he shouted, his control slipping. "*Now*, when they're worked up by the rioting . . . at their most bloodthirsty!" His anger was palpable as a sudden flame in the room.

Solita backed away from him, pressing herself against the tall bureau behind her. Her face, now white and pitiful, was drained of its recent angry red. "Darling . . . !" It was her little girl voice, pathetic and appealing. "What else could I do but send for the police, thinking Molly had been silly enough to let one of our keys get into the hands of revolutionaries? I've given her plenty of time to get it back, but when this strike started and things began to look black I felt I could no longer wait to do something about the missing key. I had no idea you had it."

"I haven't," Martin said coolly.

Solita drew a quick breath. "But you told that policeman . . ." Words failed her, the enormity of Martin's perfidy swamping her role of sweet helplessness. "You would commit perjury to save this wretched girl," she cried, "who in her cheap little way has been doing all she could ever since she came to attract your attention. Her one aim has been to make trouble between us . . ."

"You can't commit perjury unless you're speaking in a court of law under oath," Martin explained with maddening exactitude. "Anyway, all I said was that I believed I knew where that key might be. That is," he turned to Molly, "if the whole of this farrago has been built up on the assumption that the key has been missing for a fortnight."

"It's at least a fortnight," Molly confirmed, "since that unlucky night I went to the Caverne, and let Claude handle the keys. After he had unlocked the gate he was dancing about the courtyard, waving the keys and shouting something silly, like 'Death to the aristocrats!' I'm sure he was only joking," she ended uneasily.

"You see!" Solita burst in triumphantly. "Is it any wonder I was worried..."

"Just a moment!" Martin put up a hand to silence her. "It's less than a fortnight since I saw those two keys on the one ring... in your own hands, Solita. It was about a week before I went to London. We had dinner in that open-air restaurant in the Bois... remember?"

Solita nodded, beginning to look less assured.

"I was using your phone, here in the salon, leaving a message with Miss Lavelle at the office. I more or less had my back to you, but there was that mirror on the wall right in front of me and I found myself idly watching what you were doing at your bureau while I was talking. You were detaching one of the keys from the ring, and you then put one key in your evening bag and the other in the top drawer of the bureau." Martin paused a moment and then moving over to the desk said, "I wouldn't mind taking a bet that it's still there." Opening the top drawer, he picked up the key and held it out in stony silence.

"One key may still be missing," Solita said breathlessly.

"There are two in the fruit bowl in the *salle-à-manger*," Molly put in. "I saw them there when I was getting lunch."

"So there are your three keys, Solita," Martin said with deadly quietness.

Solita assumed an air of astonishment and innocence. "I had no idea the third key was in that bureau drawer, Martin... honestly!"

"A drawer you use constantly. Where you keep your daily correspondence, your engagement book..." His voice rose. "Of course you knew the key was there, where you'd deliberately hidden it. It's no use lying to me, Solita. You're a dangerous woman, capable, it seems, of going to any lengths to protect your monstrous ego. Molly was in some way a challenge to you, and you couldn't bear that. You've had it in for her for long enough..."

"Ever since you started amusing yourself with her, playing her off against me," Solita retorted, her spirit returning. "It's the sort of thing some men enjoy... you were trying to make me jealous. It gave you a sense of power over me which you couldn't get in any other way."

"Okay," Martin shrugged. "If that's what you want to believe. But even supposing it were true it didn't give you the right to concoct this horrible little plot against Molly. You must have started it when she gave herself away, chatting to you about her student acquaintances, and how one of them amused himself trying to make stink bombs—something lots of kids in science labs do. What I can't get over is the cold-blooded way you built it all up and were preparing to hand her over to the police. A stranger in a strange land ... what chance would she have had? Conspiring with revolutionary students! People are being thrown into prison for far less every hour of these troubled days." The words choked him. "You make me sick!" he cried. "Only someone utterly wicked—or badly deranged—could have acted as you've done!"

"I'm certainly not deranged," Solita muttered sullenly. Then with another flash of spirit, "You're the one who's deranged, rushing back from London in the midst of a General Strike because you thought your precious Molly was in a spot of bother!"

"She *is* my precious Molly," Martin said, and moving to her side, put an arm about her. It couldn't be happening, Molly felt. This was all some fantastic dream from which she would presently waken. But there was nothing dreamlike about the substantial shoulder against which she found herself leaning.

"I had warned her," Martin was saying to Solita, "to contact me if she ever became frightened of you in one of your incalculable rages."

"You did *that*!" Solita shrilled. "You talked to her like that about me behind my back when you were supposed to be engaged to me... What loyalty!"

"I wasn't judging you, Solita. I know you suffered a severe nervous breakdown after I left you in New York last year... for which I blamed myself bitterly."

"It was not a nervous breakdown!" Solita's tone was defiant. "You misunderstood something I said to you that evening we first met again here in Paris, and I let it go, wanting to make you suffer. I felt it served you right after the way you'd treated me... but I knew you loved me all the time and that I could easily get you back if I wanted you. The two months I spent in a nursing home after our historic row was because I'd strained a muscle in my heart doing those enormous canvases... all the reaching up and stretching and climbing about. So I had to rest. It was heart strain, my dear Martin, not heartbreak. I'm not the type to indulge in a broken heart, or in a nervous breakdown." Confidence was returning to her visibly as she went on. Drawing herself up straight and proud, she gave him her brilliant hypnotic glance, slowly smiling. "I knew you would come back to me, my dear. Then you turned up here in Paris..."

"And you started pulling the strings," Martin supplied. "Well, you've pulled them a little too hard this time... and they've broken. The fact that you don't suffer from heartbreak makes it easier for both of us, doesn't it?

"So I'll take Molly and go." He looked down at her,

removing his arm from her shoulder. The tender concern in his eyes made her feel a little dizzy. "Are you ready for the take-off?" he asked.

She nodded. "My bags are already packed." The dream was becoming more and more unbelievable!

"Then let's pick them up and get out."

He went with her down the corridor, Solita following them. "You didn't really think I would have let that *flic* take Molly away for interrogation, did you, Martin?" she pleaded.

Not answering her, he went into the bedroom and collected the two suitcases, Molly keeping close to his side, still hardly able to believe she was really getting out of this nightmare apartment.

When they came into the hallway Solita was standing beneath her glaring Solomon Islanders, beside the rubber plant, blocking their exit.

"Martin!" All her powers of pleading were in the softly spoken name. "Let's talk this out quietly... alone. We've both said things to each other just now that I'm sure we didn't mean. We can't just end it all like this. Darling, you *know* we can't. We belong together...we're in each other's blood..."

She was Solita at her most irresistible once more, her charm at its most feminine and alluring. Her cruelty to Molly over the keys, her sending for the police... all this could be wiped out by the flutter of her long curling lashes, the pleading in her magnificent eyes.

But this time the charm didn't work. Just for an instant when Martin put the suitcases down, she thought she had won, and Molly saw the flash of naked triumph light up her beautiful face. But he had only freed himself of the luggage so that he might take her gently but firmly by the shoulders and move her out of their path. He did not speak to her again as, having picked up the bags once more, he followed Molly into the tiny lift.

Running after them, Solita held on to the stationary grilled gate as the cage slipped away and began its descent. Though she was mouthing something, they could not hear what she said, and Molly would never forget the look of frenzied rage on her face as they vanished from her sight.

Taking a handkerchief from his pocket, Martin wiped his brow. "Phew! What a woman! Let's get away from this place as quickly as we can. I've got an office car waiting outside . . ." He put a finger under her chin and tilted it, searching her face. "Molly of the silences," he said. "Molly my quiet one! What a relief you are . . . what a blessed return to sanity." And still she couldn't find the words in which to answer him. This dream that wasn't a dream, but the electrifying truth.

"Oh, Martin!" she managed at last, "I can't believe it! You've really come to help me to get away . . ."

"Just that," he said. "And so much more!"

They were in the car by this time, crossing the Concorde bridge. "Let's go and collect our senses in your beloved Tuileries," Martin suggested. "I can park the car down one of the side streets off the Rue Royale."

It wasn't until they were sitting under a towering chestnut tree that sustained conversation became possible.

But for a time they sat in silence. Neither of them seemed to know just where to begin. It was Molly who said at last, a little formally: "It was awfully good of you to come all this way to rescue me today. How did you manage to get away from the office?"

"I just up and walked out," Martin replied.

And he told Solita I was 'precious', Molly thought. He had put his arm about her—simply in an access of sympathy, perhaps. Or could it have been to strengthen his rejection of Solita, arousing her antagonism?

Has he been just using me once more; this time to

187

help to disentangle himself from Solita's clutches? Molly wondered, and pushed the unworthy suspicion away. Martin was well and truly finished with Solita Gerard this time. She didn't dare to speculate as to what he thought about herself.

"The moment I spoke to Miss Lavelle this morning," he was saying, "I knew I had to get over here in double quick time. I could feel in my bones that something pretty drastic was happening to you, and that your call to the *Clarion* for help was really a call to me."

He slid an arm along the back of the seat. "Dear Molly! It hasn't been easy these past weeks, watching the way Solita treated you, and finding myself more and more tied up with her. I was worried by the crazy pictures she's painting, the nervous breakdown she pretended to have had—pinning it on me, filling me with guilt. Oh, she's fooled me along all right! Manipulating me the way she tries to manipulate everyone who crosses her egotistical path. But I didn't see through it until that day at the Japanese theatre with its cleverly manipulated puppets, and you pointed out how people in real life can be as easily manipulated by someone unscrupulous. Even then I couldn't break free from Solita in case she should try to injure herself—she had actually threatened to kill herself if I didn't fall in with her plans—and while I didn't take this threat seriously I was afraid she might harm herself in some way." He paused. "In the event it was you she tried to harm..."

"She couldn't help it," Molly found herself defending Solita, thinking of her alone now with her defeat in that dark, cheerless apartment. "She's in love with you."

Martin shook his head. "I wouldn't call it love, exactly. It's her iron will, not her heart, that rules her actions. And she happened to want me—the way she might decide she would like to have a summer home in the Bahamas, or a new expensive car." He broke off with a shrug. "But let's not waste any more time talking about her. Let's talk about ourselves. I've got to leave for London tonight, and you're coming with me, aren't you? Is it that you have to get home suddenly, or were you running away from Solita?"

"Running away from Solita," Molly admitted a little shamefacedly. "I was scared when she said she was sending for a policeman to come and interrogate me about the missing key. Then when I set off with my two suitcases I met strike notices at every point. It was very frustrating, and I was afraid to go back to Solita, though I plucked up my courage and did in the end. Literally I had nowhere else to go!"

"You poor kid!" The arm along the back of the seat now more warmly enclosed her. "What you've been through today!"

"It hasn't been very pleasant," Molly agreed. "And I'd love to go back to London with you tonight, but I'm wondering now if I ought to leave Uncle John in the middle of a General Strike." She told Martin then about her uncle's seizure. "Do you think I ought to remain in Paris and look after him?" she asked.

Martin's, "No", was very definite. "He'll be perfectly safe in his nursing home. Hospital services will be maintained, it has been announced. So will food supplies. The French aren't going to be done out of their grub! So it isn't a hundred per cent solid, this strike, and I doubt if it will last very long."

"That's all right then." With a sigh of relief Molly settled down a little more comfortably in the curve of Martin's arm—an easy, casual embrace. She mustn't read too much into his quixotic dash across the Channel to rescue her. Distances meant nothing to a modern newspaperman, even in the middle of a General Strike, and he had always taken a comradely interest in her affairs.

"It's going to be a bit peculiar at home without Mother," she mused aloud. "But I'll soon get busy, find myself another job."

"I can think of one right now that's crying out for you," Martin said. Something in his tone made her heart miss a beat.

"There's a lone newspaper correspondent," he went on, "who is very tired of trying to get along on his own ... coping with housekeeping problems, to say nothing of more serious matters, like Anglo-French-American sirens. What would you say to taking him under your wing, Molly bawn?"

She wondered if she had heard aright, her eyes full of questions as she faltered, "Oh, Martin!" and found herself instantly lost in an embrace that was by no means casual. And because it was springtime in Paris, nobody minded, not a head turned to look at them. Strikes might come and go, police *wagons* scream up and down the boulevards, but lovers still kissed under the chestnut trees, pigeons strutted over the green grass; the inevitable children rolled their hoops, and the old man carrying balloons wandered down the green avenues in his endless dream.

When they surfaced after a timeless interval, during which the whole of Molly's world turned upside down in an unimaginably glorious somersault, they sat looking at one another with that air of newly found wonder which only lovers can achieve.

"Oh, Martin!" Molly sighed once more. "I never thought I could matter to you like this."

"The point is, how much do I matter to you?" Martin asked, dropping a light kiss on the tip of her nose.

"So much ... so much," she whispered. "Didn't you guess?"

"I didn't dare to guess. I was in no position to speculate as to how you felt about me, involved as I was with Solita. I could only watch over you from a distance, hoping all would be well with you. But I couldn't help worrying about you, knowing how much Solita disliked you, and how ruthless she could be. I think she sensed from the start what I felt about you and it was a deep affront to her pride ... she just couldn't take it."

"It wasn't as if I was anyone dazzling or interesting," Molly said humbly. "If I could have been a more worthy rival ..."

Martin threw back his head and laughed. "Oh, Molly, I adore you!"

Molly shook her head in honest bewilderment. "I can't think why. I'm so ... ordinary."

It was then he said almost roughly, "Let's go somewhere I can really kiss you. Maybe that will make you understand what you mean to me." He made a baffled gesture as if words failed him. "You're so made of truth ... so real. If only I hadn't wasted two years realising it what a lot of trouble might have been saved. But we'll make up for it, my darling." He drew her to her feet. "There's my flat not very far away, and apart from that kiss I'm going to give you, we've got to find ourselves a meal before we set off to drive to the airport. Not Orly," he added. "There are no planes leaving Paris tonight, so it will have to be Brussels. It will be a long journey for you, I'm afraid."

"I don't care how long it is if I'm travelling with you," Molly sighed blissfully.

He tucked her hand through his arm. "Let's go, then, my love." He looked down at her purposefully. "And may this be the beginning of a journey that will last us the rest of our lives!"

Have You Missed Any of These
Harlequin Romances?